Change Gonna Come

by

Cheryl Miles

About The Book

This book looks at war through the eyes of an orphaned Gullah slave girl circa 1862, after the fall of South Carolina to the North, during the American Civil War. She has survived the horrors of enslavement and finds herself one Sunday morning fleeing a rampage of southern whites, desperate to find her way to a school for freed slaves run by a Northerner, on St. Helena Island, South Carolina.

Following the obscure directions from her recently deceased father, the story documents her long and harrowing journey. She takes shelter in a flea-infested lean-to, eating whatever food she can scavenge. Befriended by a privileged white child, she is soon compelled to flee once more through a war-ravaged countryside, encountering rebels, traitors, disease, and deadly skirmishes that threaten her survival.

Her story is one of endurance and determination, her transformation from an uneducated Black Gullah slave into a gifted writer, doctor, and activist. Her story is a plea to look beyond a privileged existence, to question accepted values and principles that separate those granted the right to self-determination from those who have no opportunity and no voice and a future as bleak as their circumstances.

Dedication

'Our most basic common link is that we all inhabit this planet. We all breath the same air. We all cherish our children's future. We are all mortal.'

John F. Kennedy

"In support of Health and Human Rights for All"

The Stephen Lewis Foundation

Grandmothers to Grandmothers Campaign

wwwgrandmotherscampaign.org

Acknowledgments

Change Gonna Come was inspired by Sam Cooke's Civil rights song "A Change is Gonna Come" and my visits to the South Carolina Sea Islands, where the Gullah people have survived slavery and its brutal consequences. The changing tides of the Lowcountry mimic the lives of a people whose circumstances rose and fell at the whim of others. If you are still, you can feel the calm of that endless rhythm, the subtle scent of the marsh's lush vegetation and abundant sea life carried in on the tide.

To Grace Cordial, Archivist at the Beaufort County Library, and the staff at the Penn Centre on St. Helena Island, who provided a comprehensive collection of historical data and information on the Gullah people and the Civil War Era, as well as the authors of reference material I used to bring this story to life,

Thank you.

Cheryl

The Angel Oak on the cover is native to South Carolina and is believed to shelter the ghosts of former slaves, whose spirits protect the tree. Blacks would hold gatherings and enjoy picnics under its giant canopy. The boat symbolizes Lucy's journey to freedom and the white building across the river is a representation of the St. Helena School for Freed Slaves (The Penn School). Cheryl was the artist who painted both the front and back covers.

The Gullah Language-A guide

Ain - and	caze - because	Duh - was, were
Ax - ask	Chimbly - chimney	Dunno - don't know
Ben - bent, bend, been	Cloze - clothes	ebn - even
Berry - very	Cohoot - bargain	Eh - he, she, it, his, hers
Bidness - business	COL'- cold	Fambly - family
Bet - best	Crap - crop	Feber - fever
Bodder - bother	excusin - except	Fren - friend
Bredder - brother	Daatuh - daughter	Fuh - for
Buckra - white man	Den - then	Fuss - first

Bun - burn

Cept - except

Haffuh - had to

Hebby - heavy

Hut - to hurt

Hankuh - long for, desire

Esef - himself, herself

Dis - just

Kine - kind

Labuh - labor

Dey - there, is, am, to be

Der - was, were, into

Most - almost

Mou - mouth

Nebbuh - never

Nuf - enough

Nuse - use, employ

Ole - old

Out - to go out

Paat - path

gimme - gave, again

Gree - agree

Ribbuh - river

Sed - sit

Sholy - surely

Staat - start

Tek - take

Tole - told

Tuh - to

Wawss - wasp

Lass - to last	Pit - put	Weh - where
Leff - to leave, left	Po - poor, pour	Wah - what, which, who
Lub - love	Pon - upon	Ya, Yo - you
Mek - make	Pusson - person	Uh - I, me
Mo - more	Quire - to inquire	Yuh - here

The Gullah language is a blend of African languages, English and Creole, influenced by cultural influences and dialects.

Seemingly unrefined to the unaccustomed ear, the Gullah tongue has been studied and recognized as a language. (1)

'Th' as in there, becomes a 'D' as in 'dere' or Brother-Bredder

'V' as in Never- becomes a 'B'- Nebbuh

'D's are often dropped at the end of words- Friend- Fren' or And- 'An'

'S'-as in Scratch- is often dropped, becoming- Cratch'

'L' will often replace a D- as well as dropped R's- Children- Chilluns'

The first two or three letters of a word are often ignored.

Except- becomes 'Cept', Neglect becomes 'Glect'

Driver-a male Black slave and responsible for the working slaves on a plantation,

Overseer-typically a White man hired by the Massa and responsible for the working slaves on the plantation.

Contents

'The Weeping Time' - Georgia 1859

The little girl sank her teeth into the wooden sill of the empty window as she watched the retreating figure of her mother. She could hear her mother's sobbing from the back of the wagon, weighted down with its shackled and weeping cargo, as it disappeared into the mist. Her screams echoed off the walls of the slave cabin, shattering the early morning calm. Familiar arms were powerless to ease her sorrow or restrain her trembling body as the little barefoot girl ran outside over the dew-dampened grass onto the dry, rutted road. Her small arms were outstretched, reaching for the fading image of her mother as her tears fell to the ground, joining those of others in front of her. Dropping to her knees, she looked skyward in supplication, pleading for the nightmare to end, but somehow knowing her prayers would not be answered.

" Don't let dem tek my Mama," she begged, her small hands pressed together in a mournful plea as a cloud of dust rose in the wagon's wake before settling like a shroud over the tiny, crumpled body.

Chapter 1-South Carolina

1862

"Run!"

Lucy prayed the endless drone of the cicadas would drown the sucking sounds of her feet as she fled along a soggy path circling the bog. A hundred yards from the praise house, she could hear the urgent pleas of her fellow slaves as she imagined the men roped together and pushed forward. She'd heard rumors, enough to know the praise house was a favored culling ground for the war. Conscription into another losing battle, another equally brutal form of slavery, another loss to her already dwindling community of aunts, uncles, and cousins. Her father had died of swamp fever only days before. Her mother was a haunting memory.

"Sunday, no be goin' to de praise house to worship. Hide in de swamp like I showed ya," her Papa had warned her days before.

"Yes, papa," she'd agreed but it was hard to leave before the singing. She loved the beatitudes, she had 'de sweedis boice ob all de chilluns', her papa used to say.

Familiar sounds, like muffled pops, shattered her train of thought, and shrill, high-pitched screams halted her progress. She turned her head toward the sounds, pop, pop, pop, then more screams.

"Dun stop. Dun look back. Ya knows de way tuh go." Her father's words bounced around in her head, concussive reminders of the beatings that she too had endured.

She kept running. More shouting and wailing. She covered her ears and started to pray silently.

'Where do uh go?'

She hesitated beside the reedy wetland, like others in the area. She drew a large round stone from her pocket and threw it into the bog; a dimpling on the surface, and in a moment, it had disappeared. She circled to the left and was on the opposite side when she stopped in her tracks.

"Where you goin', little bird?"

The deep voice was familiar, and Lucy imagined the fat, red, and heavily jowled face of Massa. She'd seen him once, but once was all she'd required. She would never forget his sickly grin and evil cussing as her father's back was shredded mercilessly with a cat-o-nines whip. Massa had never been seen again on his land until now; it seems he 'd caught the fever but had survived. He did not know the sea islands of the Carolinas well, nor had experience with the many ways one can die here. She turned to face him, and the heavy rifle slung over his right shoulder.

"You're a ripe one. Come back here, there's nowhere to go."

"Ya gonna hab tuh catch me fuss, Massa."

"Sassy thing, you'll pay for that."

"Already hab, Massa."

She hid behind an angel oak, Spanish moss draping from its low-slung branches touching the soft, peaty soil beneath her feet. She zigzagged through the dense undergrowth, running through the woods, trying to avoid the line of fire. She felt a sharp stabbing pain in her right arm but kept on until she reached the next tree. Hiding behind it, she watched as the big man stepped forward, rifle held out in front, eyes fixed straight ahead on his target. One, two, three steps; he was still upright. The young girl continued to stare and pray silently.

"Sweet Jesus." It was more of a grunt than a plea as if all air had escaped his lungs.

She watched in rapt attention as the big man struggled to move his legs and reach for purchase at the tall reeds that were beginning to close in on him as his feet disappeared beneath him. The gun lay on the surface and seemed to maintain its position even as Massa was losing his.

"Help me, please. Dear God, help me."

His screams faded with every step she took, as she ran along the ragged and overgrown scrub path towards what she hoped were the warm waters lapping at the distant shores of St. Helena. God wasn't listening to the slaver today. He was too busy bearing witness to the earthly suffering of his devoted servants back at the praise house. She didn't need to get closer to confirm her worst suspicions. She'd witnessed this before. Men and boys marched away to some other God-forsaken place, never to be heard from or seen again. She moved deliberately through the marshland, stepping carefully around the sucking bog that had claimed more than a few victims over the years. At twelve, Lucy was smaller than most girls her age, thankfully, but was terrified of the curves that had started to define her transition to womanhood. She bound her chest and wore loose skirts cast off from women twice her age. Babies meant more slaves and more money and more grief when they were wrenched from your breast, often dying before their second birthday. It wasn't just the Massas she feared. The black drivers could be just as brutal.

The sunlight was fading by the time she reached the ancient oak cloaked in so much Spanish moss it was difficult to recognize the abandoned slave hut that leaned precariously beneath it. Its roof seemed ready to collapse in upon itself. The soil was sandy here and the door that hung by a single rusty hinge creaked its objection as she pulled it towards her. She quickly scanned the interior, which appeared empty except for a torn quilt partially covering a wooden crate and a shattered baby cradle that occupied a far corner where the roof had intruded. She ducked her head through the opening and bent forward as she stepped inside and stood up. Her eyes darted from side to side, senses on high alert for any signs of life; she had a deathly fear of snakes. Cottonmouths had taken the life of more than one slave on her plantation. (2) She grabbed a stick from the earthen floor and lifted the blanket slowly, revealing a roughhewn box. She removed its lid to reveal a chipped cup and metal tin inside. As she reached for the cup, a large black spider clinging to the inside appeared, and the frightened girl stifled a scream as the hairy, leggy black creature scurried away under the door.

It took a moment before she was able to breathe again. She searched her little domain until satisfied she was alone. She twisted the rusted lid on the tin and peeked inside. A dried ear of corn and some hard biscuits were wrapped in a thin cloth. She'd need some water from the nearby stream before she could swallow her next meal. She had secreted a dried apple and a crumbling molasses cookie inside the pocket of her skirt. She would eat the fruit now and save the biscuit and corn for breakfast.

She listened at the door before venturing outside. She went to the narrow stream behind the hut and filled the cup. The water tasted fresh. She hadn't seen any people or other structures on her circuitous path to this refuge that might have tainted it. Back inside, she spread out the blanket and removed the cookie from her pocket. She dipped it into the cup and waited; a moment later, she bit into her supper and, for the first time since her father had died, inhaled deeply, then releasing her breath, slowly clasped her hands together in a silent prayer of thanks. She listened to the drone of the cicadas beyond her temporary refuge.

"Ouch!"

She felt a bite on her leg. After inspecting the blanket, she decided to rid it of any other annoyances. Grabbing it, she went outside and struck it repeatedly against the oak. She inspected it for any more spiders or bugs. Hoping there were none remaining, she returned to her shelter and spread the thin quilt over the uneven earthen floor. She turned it over to take a closer look at what once must have been colorful patches, faded now. Intricate designs, she'd seen slave women painstakingly piece together from scraps of dishcloths and fabric remnants, depicted log cabins, dippers, wagon wheels, wrenches, bowties, and evening stars. They were joined with precise stitches as if a story was being told or a mystery to be solved; sometimes, the stitching was elongated, resembling a path. 'Quilt codes' was the term the slaves used to describe these blankets. She remembered seeing one hanging from a clothesline one evening, but the next day it had disappeared. (3)

She wrapped the ends around her slender torso and arms, strangely comforted by the memories it evoked. She tucked her chin into her chest and stretched the ragged quilt over her head, hoping it would minimize the biting annoyance of the sand fleas. A sharp pain in her left arm alarmed her. Rubbing it with her right hand, she was surprised to see a streak of red staining her palm. Blood? Then she remembered the rifle. In her panic, she had forgotten about the shot that had been directed at her and had grazed her arm. She felt the area again, but the bleeding had stopped. She would clean it in the morning. Time to get some rest now. A fire would have been a blessing, but blessings were in short supply this Sabbath. Even so, she said a silent prayer of thanks and humbly asked for deliverance. The war would end soon. She'd heard the rumors. Her father had warned her to keep vigilant. When men speak of war ending and freedom for slaves, it is the time to be wary of retribution and bitterness. Violence would be exacted on the slaves and those foolhardy enough to defend them. He had told her about the safety of a school on St. Helena for freed slaves and to 'flee der if de Massas start de killin'.'

She closed her eyes. The cicadas' song, though strong, wasn't sufficient to drown out the screams and the steady report of gunshots that had once again started their incessant chorus inside her head. She stuck her fingers in her ears and began to recite the Beatitudes, hoping the devil would hear and retreat.

"Blessed are de poor in spirit, for ders is de kingdom of heaben; blessed are dey dat mourn, for dey shall be filled…" (4)

She rocked back and forth until she could rock no more, praying for silence, then fell backward. Her head made contact with the blanket and earth and something hard. She released a piercing scream that jarred the chaos in her brain, and suddenly her unseen companions were silent. The devil's errand complete, he departed. Alone again, she dared to imagine freedom in a place called St Helena.

Chapter 2

"Dear Jesus, what hell be dis?"

Choking back his vomit, bare feet trudging through layers of coal dust, Henry was just another freedman in a long line of hunched, blackened bodies shuffling down a narrow shaft. His last memories were of shading his eyes from the noonday sun; its harsh glare reflected off a courthouse window as a white judge, a local landowner, stated he would be working off his debt in the mines. Thirty days, he had heard. Who could last even one?

A shovel in his hands, urgent commands to fill the coal cars, and the sharp report of a cracking whip, like a bullet ricocheting off the walls, constantly ringing in his ears. Five tons of coal a day.

'How do I measure dat? De whip reminds me. De dey must be over. I sees another body being loaded out of de shaft an into de coke oven, jus 'nother nameless freed slave. I tink slavery was hell.

If Hell has a name, it be emancipation.

If Hell has a place; it be here.

I no longer fears hell.

I prays for death.

Light ahead. 'I feel like a dead man walking, but I cannot stop; so many behind an ahead of me. Uh hears a roar ain de earth shudders 'neath my feet. A noxious tide of bodies movin' to de fading light ain coal dust like a black fog smoderin me.'

Outside, Henry feels himself being pushed aside, then falling and tumbling, over and over, gaining momentum like a runaway coal car, speeding down an incline, sharp points piercing his sides as rocks and low shrubs scrape his skin. Another explosion. Where daylight was a moment ago, it is now as dark as night. He sees fire in the distance. A siren sounds. Then nothing....

He opens his eyes. How long has he lain here? He is covered in thick black mud and ash. A train sounds its whistle in the distance. He sits up, gets to his knees, and stands unsteadily. He looks around; he is in some sort of gulley. The familiar sounds of steel on tracks persist, and he moves in its direction under the large, faded crescent of a new moon. Stumbling along, feeling the sudden cooling of rushing water as it reaches his knees, his waist. A river? He forms a cup with his hands and scoops up the liquid, lapping like a wild dog, again and again. He can taste the acrid residue of coal dust and dips his body into the water, this time scraping the black soot from his face with the tail of his threadbare shirt. He stumbles up an embankment and the earth shudders, as the train continues to rumble along, getting closer and closer until he can see the conductor's head at the window. It starts to slow down as it rounds the bend where he is lying low, out of view, he hopes. It passes him, and his eyes follow the long chain of coal cars as it continues to snake slowly along the rails. It goes on endlessly, and despair begins to dull his senses once again, where hope dwelled a few short minutes before. He climbs the embankment, gripping sparse scrub brush with his calloused hands. Suddenly, the snake appears to have a large square head, and he recognizes redemption as he runs alongside a freight car, grabs onto the bar, and hauls himself on board. (5)

Chapter 3

Lucy awoke with a start, opening her eyes slowly to an inky darkness as she lifted the blanket off her face and clutched it to her chest. Curled into the smallest form she could manage, disoriented and shivering, she froze, too terrified to move, as a scratching noise sounded at the door. She peeked out and saw a long tail scurrying under the gap.

"Be still," she scolded herself. "It only be a mouse."

Her mouth was dry as a cotton boll when she suddenly remembered the stream from the night before and collected the cup from the top of the crate. She rose slowly and headed towards the door. Squeezing her narrow frame between the gap and the door jamb, she angled her head just enough to survey the outside. Dampness glistened off sea oats, whose creamy spikes nodded in response to the prevailing wind. Persistent stringy tentacles of periwinkle clung to her shelter with vise-like grips as a skittish gecko slid away into the underbrush at the young girl's movement. Satisfied she was alone, she exited and stood upright. She heard the familiar gurgling and followed the sound with a cup in hand. She bent down and drank her fill, wiping the drips from her face with the back of her hand before refilling the crude container. Tea would be nice.

She laughed at the absurdity of the idea. Why not a nice hot corn biscuit and honey, too, as if wishing could make it so? She pushed up her sleeve and leaned over, splashing water on the gash on her arm. She was surprised to see that it had obscured her branding. 'Strange,' she thought, smiling to herself, that the musket ball intended to return her to her enslaver had eliminated his mark of ownership.

She listened for any sound or movement; footfall, voices, dogs, scythes chopping at the underbrush, loose chains. White man talk. Wary, immobile, and, except for short periods of somnolence, alert. The dampness of the night hung in the air and dissipated as thin shards of sunlight pierced the ragged gaps in the partially collapsed roof. When she finally dared to raise the scratchy blanket off her body, dust motes, caught in the morning light, danced in the air around her head. She scratched behind her ears and at her ankles and felt the familiar itching lumps. She wished she had the medicine woman's salve that her daddy had traded his wooden carvings for. It worked like magic against those sand devils. She redirected her attention to her surroundings, straining to detect any movement or distant murmurings. Her daddy always said she had the ears of a cat. The gentle sigh of the river as it met the shore in the distance was the only sound, she heard except for the rumblings of her stomach, reminding her that she needed more than just

shelter to survive if she was to reach her
destination.

She dried the cleaned gash on her arm with
the sleeve of her shirt and waited for more
bleeding. None materialized. She eyed an
everlasting plant with its straggly white flowers
and stems; she crushed some and applied them to
her bites. The itching abated. She was about to
stand and return to the shelter when she heard the
crunch of disturbed underbrush. Terrified, she
froze. A squirrel, scavenging the ground beyond
her hideout, scurried past her, his cheeks swollen
with acorns, then disappeared up the trunk of a
large oak. She let out a long sigh of relief.

She leaned her back against that same
ancient oak and slid into a sitting position at its
base. Spanish moss, draped over the branch
above her head, mottled the light that escaped
through its wispy lace and painted the ground
with an artful abstraction. The rough bark
scratched her bare legs and the damp from the
moist groundcover seeped through the folds of
her skirt. She realized she hadn't relieved herself
since she'd escaped the plantation the day before.
She crouched raising her skirt, and as her stream
began, felt the warm pungent liquid escape,
cascading onto the soil beneath. She waited until
she had finished, then rose again to survey her
surroundings.

'Where does uh go?'

The school was on the island of St. Helena and had been told a white woman was providing learning for black children. Could it be true? Tales had been told over the campfires at night, but her father had assured her that it was no lie; freed slaves would be taught and boarded for free. Free! That was something she could not believe, no more than the freedom that had been promised with one white hand and taken back, brutally, with the other. She'd heard that some dispossessed land owners and rebels were prowling the plantations, praise houses, and fields, killing freed slaves, and looting and burning homes without fear of reprisal. Who was she, a scrawny slave girl, to expect anything different from a strange woman, a white northerner at that? Rumor had it that The North had won the war here in South Carolina, and that was supposed to mean slavery was gone. Someone had forgotten to tell the Massas, who had killed her fellow slaves and razed their homes and praise houses. She had no alternative but to keep moving. Once she reached the river, she needed to continue east and cross to the other shore.

'Follow de sun an keep it at yo back when de night falls til' yo reaches de shallows. Dun cross alone. Someone will git yo.'

Who that someone might be was a mystery but that was all she had to go on. The sun penetrated her exposed skin as she walked parallel to the distant shore. She hoped to find shelter by nightfall and if not; best not to think of that. Don't tempt the devil with maybes.

What other choice did a runaway slave have?

She followed a well-worn path as the sun rose in the sky until her feet were sore and her stomach began its relentless gnawing. She felt the beads of perspiration track down her forehead and decided to take refuge in the shade of the forest canopy. She moved into the woods and sat down on an old stump that held the remnants of acorn shells. She brushed those aside and wiped her brow with the hem of her blouse.

She heard shouting in the distance and the sharp yelp of a dog. She crouched and froze instinctively, praying for the moment when the barking would fade along with the voices. In the distance, a young girl wearing a wide brimmed hat, was leaning over, and tugging at something, she then placed in a sweetgrass basket. (6) She appeared to be standing in a garden surrounded by a makeshift fence, but the scene was partially obscured by the tall grass screen ahead of her. She crept forward, slowly threading her way through the foliage, careful to keep a safe distance. She caught a glimpse of long, feathery greens hanging over the brim of the basket; likely carrots were attached at the other end. The little harvester turned her back to the voyeur and raised her head as she responded to a call. She waved her hand in the air above her head.

A white hand. Someone had beckoned to the young girl as she raised her basket above her head and pointed. She turned briefly in the direction of the stranger. As if dodging a bullet, the little slave fell to the ground and held her breath. She peeked through the tall grass, praying that she had not been seen, prepared to remain fixed in her present location until discovered or the way was clear to carry on, whichever came first. She waited.

The sun was moving west in its predictable arc in the afternoon sky, as she rose and moved slowly toward the area where the white girl had picked the vegetables. She remained in a crouched position, moving steadily through the thick grass. She split the thick vegetation with both hands and stared at the lush garden ahead of her, her eyes fixed on some scattered vegetation strewn about. She regarded the cache with trepidation and, looking around, moved forward. On closer inspection, she recognized the familiar ochre, the bumpy shape of yam, and the narrow orange tapers of carrots. She quickly filled her skirt with the unexpected treasure and walked swiftly toward the copse of trees and, hopefully, shelter in the distance.

She needed to find some water to clean the brown soil from the fresh root vegetables. She moved away from the path the stranger had taken, careful not to upset her newly harvested treasure. The trees ahead seemed a likely place to hide out of view, but she needed to make certain she was a good distance from the house of the girl who had fled to the call of her mammy, perhaps or mother. Her clothes had been tidy and trimmed with lace, certainly not those of a slave or servant child. What chance did she have to be accepted with her sudden and unkept appearance. Or her color. Or her branding, such as it was. She knew very well the mean ways of Massa's children. More than one transgression had been transferred to her bare back. She had become very careful to keep a respectful distance from the children, occupying herself with house chores and weeding the vegetable gardens and flower beds.

She spied a small brook on her left, bordered by an irregular rocky ledge. Bending over, Lucy emptied the carrots onto a mossy outcrop, then carefully separated the delicate green stems from their base. She cupped her hands and drank the water greedily until she'd had her fill, then turned her attention to the orange tapers and the yam, swishing them in the running water and watching as the crumbling brown sediment disappeared downstream. She took a hesitant bite of a carrot and, relishing its sweet tartness, took another. And another. The second was dispatched as quickly as the first. The yam, though tasty, was tough, and she struggled to finish it as she sat back on her heels and looked around. A flash of red caught her attention, out of place in this inland sea of greens and yellows. She turned her head to one side to verify the sighting, but it had disappeared. She stood hesitantly as if expecting to be discovered and moved along against the flow of the stream, carefully scanning the area and cradling the remaining carrots in her skirt. Clouds obscured the sun momentarily and she shivered, goosebumps erupting on her arms with the sudden change in temperature, an unexpected break from the heat of the past few days.

She walked for a few minutes more before noticing a large building in the distance. A line of oak trees framed the path leading up to the wide verandah and entrance. She stared at the lovely house; intricate wood patterns framed the verandah and hugged sturdy columns at the top, continuing across the roof line at the entrance to the home.

"Pretty, isn't it?".

The remaining carrots spilled onto the scrub path landing with a soft 'plop', accompanied by a sharp intake of air as the little girl stopped midstride, immobilized by a familiar dread. This time, she was on foreign soil, as foreign as Angola, the birthplace of her father, as dangerous as any she'd known.

"What's your name?"

The high-pitched tone was sweet, angelic almost. Those were the deadliest; the lilting, soothing entreaties, easy to fall into those traps.

"I'm Emma," she said, pointing in the direction of the plantation house. "Where do you live?"

Silence. Terrified to identify herself, terrified of another whipping or worse. She was a runaway slave girl. Worthless to most Massas unless…

"I won't tell anyone you're here. Did you get lost? I can have my Daddy take you home. Don't worry."

Worry? Fear, dread, terror, yes; worry was a luxury she'd never known. Worry was for white folk's problems, like a rip in a dress, spoiled milk, or a sick child, but not for slaves, who were as common as sand flies. One bite and wham, you were gone.

"I can help. I have a place where you can stay. No one will know you're there. If you don't tell me who you are, I'll have to tell my Mama about you. If you're an escaped slave, then you'll be in real trouble."

Silence.

"We had a slave girl like you once. She was my friend. We used to play together when no one was looking. But she was taken away and sold. I miss her. You could be my new friend. We could play and I wouldn't tell anyone. I promise."

It was a sincere plea, she could tell. She knew she should move on, but she had no idea where she was going. Maybe this girl knew. She could talk to her and find out what she needed to know and then leave. She could give her a name; it didn't have to be hers.

"What's your name?"

"Molly." She blurted out her mother's name; less chance of being identified as an escaped slave named Lucy.

"That's a lovely name. Molly. I like it. Are you lost? I love stories about girls getting lost and then being found by handsome princes. Don't you?"

Lucy knew no such stories about princes, handsome or ugly. The only story she knew was of Brer Rabbit and Brer Fox that her daddy had told 'round the fire at night. There was always a moral at the end; like don't pretend to be something you're not or steal or lie.

"Uh s'pose."

"We have an abandoned barn, not far from here, in the woods. You could stay there. I could bring you some food. We could tell stories and play house with my dolls."

Lucy thought about the alternative. She was so tired. She wanted to lie down and sleep so badly. Maybe just one night.

"Emma?" The shout came from the direction of the big house.

"Coming Mama." Emma turned to her new friend Molly.

"I must go. The shelter is at the far end of this path. See the tall tree bent way over? Walk a spell beyond that towards the river, and you'll see it. It's open. If not, there's a key under the rock beside the door. We stored hay there. Don't worry; no one goes there anymore. The horses are all gone. The soldiers took them. I'll bring you some food in the morning. Promise me you'll stay?"

"Uh, promise."

"Emma!" The voice was getting louder and nearer.

"I'm on my way, Mama."

Emma ran across the path lifting her full skirt as she went, the swishing of crinolines, the only sound that separated the two girls at this moment, a sound that Molly's clothes never made.

Lucy had known only 'slave cloth,' a new dress allotted twice a year made of a linsey, a cotton-wool blend, one yard per child and seven for each woman, sewed by the slaves. There was talk of something new called a sewing machine; you could make a seam in less than a minute. Who could believe that? Needles and thread were all she'd ever seen or used. She had used scraps of cloth that Massa's wife had thrown away to make clothes for her doll, Lady. Lucy liked to trim the aprons of the women slaves with bits of indigo cloth. She remembered the blue stains from the dye on the hands of the housemaids years ago before the Massa stopped growing the crop. Cotton bought more slaves. But Lucy had to be careful. If the children of Massa thought the slave clothes were too pretty, they were quick to report the offending item. She remembered trimming her first petticoat with blue ruffles and fashioning a headscarf of the same fabric. Massa's children were quick to report her felony to their mother; the sound of the scissors slicing through her petticoat and head wrap cut far deeper than any beating she could remember. But memory was a weapon that she had learned to hone, unseen and ever present, like a cottonmouth before it struck.

She was eager to be free. No more 'plantation cloth' for her. She loved colorful clothes and was eager to cast off the fabric shackles to defy the laws forbidding slaves to dress above their station. She would go to school. She would open her own shop and order beautiful cloth from the North. There were rumors of free black women owning their own dress shops. One day, she would, too. Clothes represented wealth and were just another way the slavers reminded slaves of their place. She knew a lot about fabrics and the restrictions imposed, but that never stopped her; she could sew better than most of the women on her plantation. (7, 39)

The countless injustices ate her soul; many of the women warned her to not arouse anger from the Massa's children with her fancy stitching. She nodded but continued tatting intricate designs in secret, saving scraps of cloth discarded by the black seamstress stored in a sweetgrass basket hidden under her bed in a corner of the cabin.

Her rebellion had started long before the war broke out.

Chapter 4

Lucy ran along the path and reached the barn, following the instructions Emma had given. Lacy moss draped over a thick live oak limb partially obscured the structure as she approached cautiously. She opened the door and entered the darkened interior. The smell of hay was overpowering at first, and she sneezed repeatedly until she became accustomed to the air. She noticed what appeared to be leather straps hanging on a wall near the door. One side of the shed was divided in two by a half wall. A large blanket was thrown carelessly atop a bale of hay. Molly retrieved it and, exiting the shed, went to the shaded rear of the structure. She held her breath and began to shake the covering with every bit of energy she could muster. She had little experience with horses; men were the ones who looked after them. She was terrified of the large beasts. She was grateful they were gone; she would have slept outside rather than share quarters with the huge, smelly, four-legged creatures.

Once inside, she found a corner of the shed that was out of view of the door. She spread the blanket on top of a bale of hay on the floor, leaning against a wall. It was far more generous than the one she had used as a cover the previous night. Reaching inside her skirt, she retrieved the dried apple and biscuit she had saved. She prayed Emma would keep her promise and return with food the next morning. She'd known hunger before but nothing like these new churning pangs that gnawed at her insides making her curl into a tight ball. She regretted eating the yam, but with no means of cooking it, she had little choice but to eat it raw. She stared at the peaked ceiling and said a prayer of thanks.

"Blessed are dey dat do hunger ain tirst..."

Light streamed in through a square window frame situated on the wall opposite Lucy's roost. She bit into the dried apple, and its sweet tartness puckered her lips. Her tongue felt thickened. She realized that if she were to continue her meal, she would need water to ease the digestion of the biscuit. The stream was close by, but it meant another foray outside. The light from the window, a few moments earlier, had faded to grey, just barely illuminating the path to the door. Another minute, and that too would disappear. She felt the biscuit in her pocket and moved to the door. She laid her head against its rough surface and held her breath while she listened for footsteps. Hearing none, she lifted the iron latch and applied gentle pressure with her hip, barely enough to wedge her hand around and grab its edge.

She froze as the hinges creaked in defiance of the sudden disturbance and listened for any sound that would signify danger. One minute, two more, perhaps; time had never been a defined element in her life. Her accounting of time lay in the rising and setting of the sun, phases of the moon, rhythms of the tide, the sowing of the crops, harvesting, prayer meetings, and visits from the Massas. A clock was for white men and their families to keep time, to go to town, to purchase more slaves, to shop, to play, to eat and sleep; allotted times for everything. A slave clock would be as redundant as three feet. Her clock would have no numbers, merely a sun and a moon. Sunrise and sunset. Time to work and time to sleep, if you were lucky- 'Day clean to first dark'- six days a week with only the Sabbath off.

She pushed the door further forward and peeked out. No sounds except the cicadas' familiar song. She moved across the path to the sounds of rushing water. Sitting on a low flat rock, she leaned over, slurping the fresh clear liquid from cupped hands. Lucy drank greedily until she felt her stomach might burst. She dipped her biscuit in the running water and ate it, once it softened. She spotted a patch of fragrant sage and picked a handful of leaves; she let them soften in her mouth and chewed them well before swallowing. That should help with any stomach cramps she might develop from eating so many uncooked vegetables.

Meal completed, she rose to her feet and retraced her steps to the shelter, treading lightly on the compacted earthen path, grateful that footprints were difficult to discern on the dried soil. Once back at the door, she gingerly lifted the latch and painstakingly pulled the handle towards her, minimizing the sounds of the rusted hinges. Satisfied no one was near, she retreated to her hiding spot, pulled the blanket over her shoulders and shivering body and closed her eyes. She knew she was in a precarious position. If Emma told her mama or papa, she would have no time and nowhere to run. Would her luck finally run out? A thought struck her.

A broom!

She needed to find a broom to lay across at the foot of the door to keep away the evil spirits of haunts, hags, and witches that stole into your bed at night and sat on your chest, causing nightmares. She looked around her little domain, searching for her salvation. She found what appeared to be a small whisk that could be substituted for a broom in one corner of a stall. It was said, by the root doctors, that the hags would be too busy counting the bristles all night to bother the occupant of the bed. She found a long stick in another corner and decided to look for some rope. A small, worn leather strap hung from a short, rusted nail alongside other broken tools on hooks, and decided it would do. She fashioned a long-handled broom, and to ensure that the makeshift talisman would work, she said a little prayer. (8).

"God bless dis broom ain keep away de debil spirits. Amen."

"Tank ya, Jesus," Lucy added quickly, remembering to thank the Lord in advance. Less chance of him forgetting a prayer from a grateful penitent. She then placed the makeshift broom at the foot of the door just touching the sill, such as it was for a shed. Still, it was better than nothing.

"Beggars caint be choosers," she scolded herself as she lay down once again onto the hay, with the blanket wrapped around her.

Curling her body into a tight ball, she closed her eyes and let her mind drift to the little white girl she had met. There was something about Emma she trusted but could not explain if asked. She seemed lonely, an odd condition for a young white girl with a mama and papa, a beautiful home and enough food to share with strangers. But she still wanted 'Molly' to play with her. 'Play house' with dolls, Emma had said. To Lucy, play and house were two words she would never use together. She had never played in the plantation house of her slavers. There was always sweeping and dusting and washing and tidying and whatever chores she was told to complete.

She had had a doll Lady', she had named it, that an Auntie had made for her one Christmas from Broom grass, with hair made from its roots. Lucy had treasured it and took it with her everywhere. Then, one day, it went missing while she was weeding the garden; she always hid it under the rose bush during the day while she was working outside. She had been desperate to find it and had searched the gardens and finally the cook house next to Massa's plantation house. She heard children's laughter, and when she peeked inside the kitchen, she saw the oldest girl throwing 'Lady' into the fireplace at the far end of the large room. Lucy had never felt such rage. It was as if all the frustration of her pathetic existence had suddenly erupted and became focused on the white girl with the lace collar and tatted apron. She ran to the fireplace, hoping to save her beloved doll from the flames that had started to consume the straw and the colorful fabric that had been lovingly stitched into a dress, head scarf and apron. She launched herself at the laughing girl who had destroyed her only, and most precious, possession. She rained punch after punch with her small, tight, and determined fists on the unsuspecting murderer until she was dragged away by the black cook responding to the children's screams.

The little slave girl had paid highly for her transgression. She had suffered the lash, and although she had witnessed many whippings before, nothing could have prepared her for the stinging, scalding pain that lasted long weeks after the insult. She was lucky she wasn't hanged, her father had said. Lucy did not feel lucky, but she did feel Lady was avenged. Somewhat. She was forced to apologize to the object of her hate, which she did with apparent contrition. The children continued to harangue her more than ever, but she never took the bait and suffered many more bruises and falls at the hands of her provokers. She appeared to have learned her lesson and after a while, the children became bored with her acquiescence. They needed fresh bait. And so, she was replaced by another slave, Joseph, a young boy with whom she had become friends, a kindred spirit.

Lucy had learned her lesson, but not one of submission- one of patience and retribution. She had had many years of observation and suffering to hone her skills. Keeping them hidden was her greatest weapon. She was no longer a frightened six-year-old. She was older, and war was brewing. The Massas were in revolt, on the losing side she had heard, against the north.

One bright sunny day, she was in the garden picking vegetables. She saw Joseph being pushed and forced to walk on hands and knees through a thick briar of scrub brush. He emerged with cuts from painful thorns all over his hands, arms, and face. The children stood laughing as he ran towards the slave quarters. She decided it was time.

She had been aware of wasps' nests not too far from the children's playhouse in the woods. One had been discovered weeks before and destroyed. The children were not allowed to return until the playhouse was cleared by the overseer. Lucy, however, knew a lot about wasps and was not afraid of them. She knew how to use smoke to calm them and how to annoy them. She also knew that they often burrowed in the ground to form nests. So, she was not surprised to find a new one in a sunken area close to the playhouse near the picnic table where the children sometimes ate their lunch. She moved the table a few feet and spread some loose brush over the nest, then spread a bit of stolen honey under the bench.

Lucy was working in the garden the following morning when she heard screams coming from the woods. Raising her head, she saw Massa's wife running, with slaves at her heels, towards the screams. Out of the woods appeared the children swatting the air and covering their heads as if chased by demons.

Stinging demons.

"Wut be happenin'?" she asked the last slave to return from the melee.

"Dey bin stung!".

"But de wawss nest be gone?"

"Dun tink so."

Lucy listened to the cries and moaning of the children for the rest of the day while they were confined to their rooms. She smiled as she dusted, cleaned, and swept floors being careful not to sing. Joseph was sitting on the stoop of the praise house the following Sunday. He was covered in ointment.

"How yo cuts?"

"Bedder. Salve helps." Joseph stared at his arms.

"Too bad 'bout de nests, "Lucy said.

"Poor wawss. Dey burn dem all."

"Strange dey return so soon."

Joseph studied his friend's face. It was devoid of any emotion or expression.

"Medicine man be out of salve fo de stings," the young boy said.

"Too bad. Glad dey was 'nuff fo yo, Joseph."

"Me too."

Joseph smiled.

Lucy winked.

Chapter 5

Henry grabbed a metal handhold and heaved himself onto the last box car of a northbound freight train. He looked briefly into the dark interior. Night descended quickly in the south, and luckily, his escape coincided with it. He sat down and leaned heavily against the wall of the car out of view of the opening and let out an exhausted sigh. It didn't matter to him where he was headed as long as it was north and away from the mines and the law, in whatever form it might take. The air reeked of old hay, horse manure and sweat mixed with the pervasive pungent scent of tobacco and moonshine, a not-so-subtle reminder that he was not alone in his choice of refuge.

As he repositioned himself against an old hay bale to allow his body some support, he felt a subtle prick in his lower back. He reached around with his right hand and swatted a mosquito that had sunk its sharp nose into his skin. He was just shy of his target and too late to arrest the bump and the accompanying itch that developed almost immediately. He massaged the area with his calloused fingers as much as he was able to and felt the familiar ragged ridges running south to his buttocks and the valley between them. Unconsciously, held his breath and closed his eyes, remembering the sounds of the whip and the rendering of his skin into jagged strips of raw flesh. He hung his head reflexively, another image replacing the first, as droplets of blood running down his legs became a stream of red as the agony continued.

"Weh yawl from?"

A voice from the darkness.

The train lurched, and the clickety-clack of the wheels rolling along the steel rails jolted Henry back to the present. He looked up and moved his head from side to side, sweeping the blackness for the source of the voice.

"Ober heah."

Henry stretched his neck to the left, his eyes focusing on a faint plume of smoke before the scent reached his nose. He couldn't discern any physical features of the body that belonged to the raspy voice, just a vague outline, but he knew he was a slave just like himself.

"Who wants ta know?" Henry was wary, nonetheless. Anonymity was his only defense, a weak one at that.

"Jeremiah. From de Putnam plantation in Georgia."

"Yo, a freed slave?" Henry asked.

A choking cough was amplified by a wheezing cackle.

"Freed? From what? Uh nearly git lynched going out wid an ole rifle uh used to hunt wild pig. White coats tek me to de lynching tree behind de plantation. Nebbuh tought Uh be happy ta see a Bluebelly coming onto my land but I shor was dat day. Attacked dem white devils long nuff for me ta run. Run faster den a fox chasin' a hen. Din know weh uh was, til I hears de train whistle. Like yo, uh jumped. Din care daylight or no."

Henry had heard stories of freed slaves, landowners even, being lynched by local white gangs. Rumors 'bout big man Forrest and the Klan, local Buckra lawmen capturing slaves for free labor, lots of money in steel and coal. He'd certainly seen his share of lynchings, but he'd thought South Carolina was a better place than Alabama. He'd heard that the Sea Islands off the Georgia coast and the Carolinas were home to Gullahs, now freed slaves, but he'd never talked to anyone who knew or had kin that lived on the islands. How could he even begin to find his way to a safe place? Did one even exist? (9).

"You 'scaped lynchin' too?" Jeremiah persisted.

"Coal mines."

"How dat?"

"De law pick me up fo loitrin' by de docks. I told dem uh was waitin' fo de boat tuh do some fishin', but dey don listen. Soon, uh was in de court an de judge says uh pays tirty dollas or go to de mines to work it off. Before I cud say Brer Rabbit uh was roped ain on de way to de prison.”

“How yo git away?”

“Din at fuss. Was sent to de Coal mines. The second day was some commotion, a fire, coal dust black as night ain everyone was runnin’ out of de mine not just slaves but whites ain Injuns too. Dere was a splosion ain uh was flyin’ in de air ain rollin’ down de hill to de muddy ditch. Was knocked out. Uh git up ain walk a ways ‘till uh falls into a stream. Uh stay in dat water ‘til my parts be shriveled like an ole hag’s. Uh got mah ropes loose ain den uh hears de train whistle. Uh runs up de hill ain haul myself on board ain here uh be.”

“Come ober here wile uh cuts off the rest of dem ropes.”

Henry shuffled across the rough, planked straw, straw-strewn floor until he was in front of Jeremiah. A small, curved blade was withdrawn from a sheath on the old man’s ankle hidden under his pant leg. Henry held out his hands, unbound but the ragged restraints still clung to each wrist. Jeremiah quickly sliced through the rough bindings and sheathed the weapon.

“Much ‘bliged. Lucky dem bossmen din have time to shackle me agin caze of de ‘splosion. Weh yo git dat knife?”

"From de cowboy dat lives down de road from my farm. Payment fo a pig. Lucky dem crackers din git it."

Henry rubbed the raised ridges of old scars and hardened callouses on his untethered wrists.

"Uh taut uh be a daid man. Not a ting ta eat since yesterday. How long can a man work wid no food?"

"Yo's lucky. Uh hears 'bout men like yo ain dey die ebry dey in de mines. Dey's chained, workin' under de eart, miles down, black holes. Fed scraps no dog wud eat. Mos die in de fuss weeks. Dey is trown out ain burned like trash in de coke obens ain newuns be brought in. Worse den on de plantations. Freed slaves? Hah. Dat's de meanness joke uh eber hear. No God-fearin' man wud bide by dat. No Suh. Dey's white debils ain dat's whose gonna' take em wen dey dies." (10)

Henry couldn't speak. He knew the mines were bad, but he was promised he'd only be there until his debt was paid. If Jeremiah was right, he'd been luckier than most. Why was the freedom he'd been promised so hard to find? Mr. Lincoln was going to pass a law that all slaves were free. Did that mean him, too? His back was starting to ache again under the weight of an uncertain future.

"Yo's young and strong. Yo can work de land ain make a life. Mebee eben tek a wife. Yo gots ta fine a place where de freed slaves is. Uh is ole; not many years left in dis body. Caint hardly walk. De moonshine be killin me. No mind. Uh ride dis train 'til I caint no more."

Henry heard a swish and a burp as a lingering odor of bootlegged liquor wafted towards him.

"Yo wants a swig?"

"No, much 'bliged. I'll git sum sleep now."

Jeremiah lifted the bottle to his mouth and drained it. He wiped a ragged gray cuff across his blue, cracked lips and sank slowly under a threadbare, coarse blanket. In a moment, the train's rhythmic swaying and the discordant rhythm of steel on steel was drowned by the thunderous chorus of Jeremiah's snoring.

Chapter 6

Lucy opened her eyes to a room flooded in light. A rooster sounded his morning reveille as she moved groggily from under the blanket and scratched at an itch in her ear.

"Debil skeeters," she said as she swatted another mosquito that had landed on her leg.

She sat upright, swinging her legs to the side of her perch, slid down onto the earthen floor littered with straw and walked hesitantly towards the exit. She bent down and moved the makeshift broom to the side, listening for any sound or footfall. Satisfied there was none, she carefully leaned her weight against the rough-hewn door and pushed gently until it moved. Peeking out in both directions, she stepped lightly onto the dew-moistened earth and headed in the direction of the stream. A rabbit scampered out of sight and disappeared into the dense undergrowth at the sudden, unexpected activity. Lucy leaned over and quenched her thirst, happy to have a clean source of water so close at hand.

A rumbling in her stomach reminded her that besides water, food was now a priority. Emma had promised to return with something for her to eat, but 'when' was the question. She remembered the vegetables from the day before and how they had fallen onto the path. She retraced her steps back towards the place where she had collected the vegetables and spied the spilt cache scattered across the path. One of the carrots had been nibbled to nothing, but another was still edible. The partially eaten yam remained. She gathered them quickly and scanned the area, fully aware that she was close to Emma's house and whoever lived inside with her. No sign of a papa. Many men had joined the army, but often, the absence of men wasn't announced. Or was lied about. Safer that way, when women were alone, she had learned. More than one woman had suffered abuse at the hands of rebels and Massas. Lucy cleaned her root vegetables in the rushing water and carried them with her to an elevated spot behind a large oak and bushy scrub, in view of the shed where she'd spent the night. Hidden from view, she bit into the carrot and savored its earthy sweetness. As she prepared to continue her meal, she heard a movement. Lucy stiffened, breath suspended, expecting the small form of Emma to appear. But the form that materialized was not that of a young girl but of a Negro man, slight of build and scantily clad, his body beaded with sweat. Visible through the ragged clothing, raised welts crisscrossed his back and disappeared into the thin, greying fabric of his trousers that clung to nonexistent hips. He sculked around to the door of the shed and looking about him, pulled on the latch, and slipped quietly inside. Lucy waited, her body rigid with fear, hoping he would soon leave after finding little value in the way of food or drink. She counted to twenty, as she had been taught by her papa, then counted again and again. Her legs began to cramp, and she felt the need to relieve herself.

Another rustling of the underbrush in the distance, and the slight form of Emma appeared. She was headed for the shed. From the stranger's nervous demeanor, he was a runaway. She knew his fate as well as her own. Her options were limited. Reveal herself and save the man from detection or flee. Emma was getting closer to the shed and had turned onto the path directly in front of it.

"Emma," Lucy called out.

Emma turned from the path towards her name. Lucy ran and intercepted her entry to the shed, placing herself between the white girl and the door.

"Hi Molly. I've brought you breakfast."

The little hostess held out a white and red striped cloth, lumpy with its contents. Emma unfurled the sides, and a wispy stream of vapor escaped, carrying with it the savory aromas of chives and jam. Lucy went to grab one, but Emma pulled the package out of reach.

"Let's eat in the shed. That way, no one will see us."

"No! "Lucy almost screamed.

"What's wrong with the shed, Molly?"

"Snakes!" She shouted without thinking, hoping Emma feared them as much as she did.

"On no. That's horrible. But don't worry. I'll get Jason to get rid of them. You're gonna be safe."

Lucy had to think fast.

"Can we eat outside? It be dusty in de shed ain I likes de sun. We kin use yo cloth ta cober de ground."

"Okay. But I'll get Jason to come later to chase those crawling demons away."

Lucy nodded. She could only deal with one problem at a time, and she prayed to find another solution to the current dilemma of the stranger. They finished half of the fresh buns and sipped on the sweet tea that Emma had placed in her apron pocket in a glass jar.

"How yo tek all dis food widout yo Mama askin' questions?"

"I told her I was having tea with my imaginary friend, like I do sometimes, except she doesn't know that you're not imaginary. Isn't this fun?"

Lucy didn't find anything 'fun' about her situation; to her, it was terrifying. Adding to her anxiety was the fact that she didn't know when the man in the shed would reappear. Would Emma report the two of them, thinking that she and he were together, both escaped slaves? She started to tremble.

"Are you cold, Molly?"

"A little. Uh din sleep much las night. Uh needs to lie down agin."

"But we haven't played dolls yet." Emma's voice had a high-pitched whine to it and Lucy knew she needed to tread carefully to not arouse suspicions.

"Uh play dolls wid you after uh has a bit of sleep. Uh be mo fun den."

"Okay, but only for an hour. I'll come back with my dolls, and we can play house in the shed together."

"Uh be here."

"See you in an hour."

Emma ran off towards the big house, and Lucy was left holding the remaining biscuits. What was her next move? Was the man friend or foe? She walked towards her hiding spot but stopped by the creaking sound of the shed door. A black head appeared, and a soft voice called gently.

"Molly?"

Lucy froze.

"Uh means you no harm. Uh be a freed slave."

"Why yo runnin' den?"

"Dey arrested me fo loitrin'. Dey sent me to work de mines. Uh 'scaped two deysago. Rode de train a spell."

"Where yo goin'?"

"Dun know. Yo belongs here?"

"Wuh diffrence dat be?"

"No diffrence." He hung his head and when he looked up again, he had tears in his eyes.

"Yo got fambly?" Lucy asked.

"All dead now."

He wiped the sweat from his forehead, and with it, streaks of dirt bruised the bags that bulged beneath his eyes.

"Too bad." Lucy looked away, refusing to allow her eyes to meet his. "Weh yo goin'?" she asked.

"Dun know. Uh be a dead man anywhere uh goes."

"But yo a freed slave. Dey caint own yo no more."

He exhaled with a forced laugh.

"Tell dat to de judge who sentenced me fo loitrin. Said uh has tuh pay tirty dollars for de costs of de trial or jail time. May as well be a tousand. Ain't got no money, if uh aint got no work. Ain free now is worse dan de slave uh was fore dey broke my chains. I hear stories bout Alabama an de steel mills, all true an' worse din dat. Yo is bound an' worked to deat, food no pig wud eat, terrible sickness in de shacks. De minute yo dies yo's trown in a coke oben to burn ain 'nother is put in yer place. Terrible, terrible evil goes on; no animal should be treated like dat."

Lucy noticed Henry staring at the food she still held tightly in her grip. Red currant jam was escaping from their middle and sticking to the sides of the cloth. The man's lips glistened as he wiped the top of his hand across his mouth. She quickly covered the savory buns and turned her head away.

This was new territory for her. She had never been in control of anything, certainly not the food. The men were always the first to eat. She was hungry and had to think about the journey ahead of her. Where she was going was still a mystery. Following the rising sun was too vague to be of help if she was faced with a river or, God help her, an ocean. She remembered her father's stories and shook her head.

"Yo hear of de school fuh freed slaves on dese islands? Run by de white woman? Fuh free?" she asked hopefully.

Blank eyes stared back. A school for freed slaves run by a white woman. There was nothing he could imagine getting free from whites except whipping. He had to be careful. He wanted food. If he pretended to know, she might share her biscuits more willingly.

"Uh tink it be furder west. On de odder island."

Lucy knew from her father that it was east, not west. But what if he had been wrong?

All she knew was that the East was where her parents had come from and the story of their journey from Africa. Weeks of travel on seas, storms spawning waves, like mountains falling onto each other, crashing onto the boat that shuddered with each assault, slamming against its sides, threatening to breach the oaken slats and wreak destruction in the hold. Hundreds of her countrymen were shackled together, unable to move from their confined spaces to attend to their toileting or hygiene for hours and days at a time. At least a breach would provide fresh air and salt water to clear the floors of body fluids or worse, dead bodies. Most of her fellow slaves did not fear water - most were good swimmers- there had been ample opportunity for swimming in the rivers and on the coast of Western Africa. The slaves brought those skills with them across the Atlantic to the plantations of the Southern States. There were many stories of Blacks saving whites from drowning. For Lucy, water was for growing crops, fishing, drinking, cooking, and cleaning. She had never learned to swim.

She turned around and stared at the stranger eyeing her biscuits hungrily and spoke in the clearest voice she could manage. She thought about what he had said. She decided she didn't trust him.

"Uh give yo a biscuit. Den yo has tuh go. Uh is friends wid de white girl. Uh be tellin' her 'bout yo if yo is still here."

The man nodded. He grabbed the proffered biscuit and ate it with such ferocity that the stunned girl stumbled backwards and landed on her rump. Before she could say another word, he grabbed at the cloth holding the last biscuit. She instinctively tightened her grip on the precious package and withdrew her hand. A shout sounded in the distance as she was about to cry out when the thief turned and ran off into the thicket. A minute later, he was out of sight, and an uneasy calm settled on the land once again. Lucy looked at the mound of biscuit and jam and began to eat the crumbled remains. Nothing would be left when Emma returned.

What do I do now?

She watched as the sun moved higher in the sky and cast an amber glow on the scrub path that led to her shelter. She was restless and torn between leaving before Emma returned, or waiting to find out something, anything, about the school from her. She had grown accustomed to deception as a matter of survival, but she was brutally honest with those she trusted. Her father always told her she was like two people in one body: sweet on the outside but sour as unripe grapes on the inside. She had never really thought about it. She had learned her lesson with her doll, Lady. Show people that you care about something, and it will be taken from you, and like Lady, you could be the next one tossed in the fire.

She felt a bead of sweat roll down her forehead and drop onto the earth below. It was going to be a hot day, she realized, standing outside with the sun beating down on her, exposed and in danger of being discovered. She ran towards the shed and slipped inside. It was warm but cooler than the air outside, thanks to the cover of trees. She lay down on her makeshift bed, shutting her eyes for a moment, waiting patiently for Emma's return. In her mind's eye, she imagined herself in a crisp, clean blouse and tunic, sitting at a desk with a slate in hand, learning her letters. The image was as soothing as a cool cloth on a feverish brow. Comforted, she slipped into a restless sleep.

Chapter 7

Lucy's body shot upright like a live ember out of a fire.

Gunfire!

Her heart was racing, ready to burst out of her chest. Paralyzed with fear, she held her breath. She could hear voices in the distance, shouting and calling out for someone to come back. She waited for another gunshot, but none materialized. What had happened? She slid off her makeshift bed, taking her blanket with her and hid between two bales of hay at the back of the shed.

'Please God, don't let them find me.'

Her prayers were interrupted by the creaking of the shed door. Shrunken into a compact fetal curl, she heard a breathy whisper as she allowed herself a glimpse of the intruder. A figure in the shape of Emma emerged, backlit from the sun streaming into her refuge.

"Molly? It's me, Emma. Are you here?"

Lucy's brain was telling her to stay hidden, but her heart was telling her to trust this young white girl.

"No one knows you're here. A runaway slave was seen on the plantation. He escaped before we could catch him. Mama tried to shoot him, but she's not very good with Papa's musket."

There was a long pause. The young black girl wondered if Emma was going to leave. How much longer could she stay hidden?

"I'm glad he got away. I think it's cruel to keep people chained up. Don't you?"

Lucy agreed. Unfortunately, she'd been tricked before by the smooth talk of privileged white children. She shrunk down further under the rough blanket. She needed to think. She closed her eyes, praying for an answer.

"Boo!"

Lucy's body jerked at the sudden noise, and the blanket fell from her face. She looked up. Her brown eyes met the unmistakable blue of Emma's.

"I knew you were in here. Why are you hiding from me?"

Too stunned to speak, she continued staring at Emma.

"Look. I brought some more biscuits."

Emma reached into her apron pocket and retrieved two pieces of cornbread. She held them under Lucy's nose. The aroma of the fresh baking overwhelmed her senses.

'You can take one."

Lucy reached for one at the same instant Emma withdrew her hand.

"Did you see that slave?"

"No."

"He was coming from this direction when my Mama spotted him."

"Uh bin sleepin'. Uh woke when uh hears dem shots."

"You were lucky he didn't see you. Mama says slaves do mean things to young girls, even white ones."

The little slave knew of many young black girls being violated by black drivers but even more by their white owners, sons, and overseers. No slave she'd ever encountered would dare touch a white girl. Lynching would be a mercy compared to some of the horrors she'd seen. The man she'd met was too hungry to be thinking of anything but his empty stomach, she was certain. Her mouth watered as she eyed the food in Emma's hand.

"Emma. Where are you?" The voice was faint but urgent.

"It's my mama. I'll come back later. Don't worry."

Before Lucy could ask for a biscuit, Emma had turned her back, biscuits still firmly in her hand, and walked briskly away without a backward glance. A stunned Lucy had nothing to still the rumblings of hunger in her stomach. The shed door was left ajar, and the humid air rushed in as Emma ran out, disappearing. Lucy was caught in a confusion of options.

Should she stay, or should she run?

She guessed that the slavers would be looking for the runaway, and she was just as likely to be caught as he. More so. She was small, alone, and afraid. Nothing had prepared her for this. She stood, and as she peeked out the window, she caught sight of Emma's retreating back when something else caught her attention. On a branch of a low shrub just off the path was the red and white napkin.

Emma saw it, too. Lucy must have dropped it in her race for the shed. Emma reached down and carefully pulled the napkin from its anchor. She stared at it for a moment before placing it inside her apron. Instinctively, Lucy retreated into the shed, trembling. Would Emma connect the freed slave to her?

Overhead, the rumble of thunder echoed her unrest. She looked skyward; an ominous grey and white cloud formation warned of the storm to come. Flooding, too, perhaps. There had been so much since the war had started. Would anybody start looking for her in this weather? She realized she had little choice. She needed the cloak of darkness to escape. She would wait.

Chapter 8

Henry had been running heedless of direction and the pounding in his chest. He looked up and recognized the cumulonimbus cloud formations of an approaching storm in the distance. He adjusted his eyes to the sun's fading brightness and studied the sun's position before the clouds obscured it. He prayed the storm would pass quickly so he could get his bearings from the stars when darkness fell. He looked down at his feet, bare of the shackles he had borne for years, his ankles calloused and scarred, indented from constant shuffling; more impressive still, they were silent.

He allowed himself the luxury of momentary reflection: his small seaside village and the sea breezes that filled his lungs and cleared his mind, his family, his betrothed. A hint of a smile softened the lines around his mouth even as his throat constricted. He had not cried since he'd been in the dank hold of the slave ship that first interminable night. He'd learned there were dangers sitting shoulder to shoulder with men bigger and more desperate than he. Food was scarce, water more so. Weeks later, women and children were dying around him from water-borne illnesses. He did not know how much longer he could tolerate the stench of vomit, urine, excrement, and death. At one point, he envied the dead.

Then redemption.

The ship's carpenter had broken his leg and died of infection. They needed a man who knew how to repair boats. When asked for volunteers, Henry had spoken loudly over the protests of other men. He would be tested; if he was lying, he would be thrown to the sharks. The alternative was not an option anymore. Death would bring relief.

He worked under difficult conditions but was rewarded with many hours spent in the open air on deck. He repaired deck boards, spars, sails, leaks in the hold, and any other task assigned. The weeks dragged on as he witnessed men, women, and children, alive and dead, weighted and thrown into the churning waters that loomed endlessly towards the horizon as disease, starvation, and water shortages exacted their toll. He wanted to save them, but their fates would become his if he tried.

. . . .

Henry's father had taught him to fish and how to read the stars to navigate his way through strange waters. What strange waters he spoke of, he had been unsure, for, as a child, his ocean forays were always within sight of the shore. But he loved the night sky and had a gift for navigation, an innate sense of direction. As he grew to be a man, he and his father ventured further into those unknown waters, returning before nightfall. His father grew to depend on Henry to bring them safely home, and, unerringly, he always did. Henry knew the signs of foul weather; he could read wave patterns, crosshatch, and cats 'paws, warnings of approaching tropical storms. The villagers depended on him to warn them of seaborne dangers. He was a very desirable man and had fallen in love with a beautiful and kind girl. They were to be married. He had been preparing his fishing dhow in the early dawn, anxious to catch the fish for his wedding feast. He savored these moments alone before dawn; his only companions were the seabirds and the gentle breeze and soothing rhythms of the ocean. He said a silent prayer of thanks, closing his eyes, head tilted skyward as the Atlantic lapped at the sandy shores of his beloved Angola. He sailed toward the horizon.

It had been a good morning; the sea had been generous. His boat was weighed down with enough fish for his wedding feast. How proud his bride would be. He leapt out of his boat and pushed it towards the beach, wondering why there was no one to greet him. He sensed danger but was unsure why.

Shouts of protest, gunfire and keening pleas shattered the calm. He was confused at first, thinking perhaps he had misheard. He waited, erect and still. The plaintive cries continued. He abandoned his boat and moved swiftly but quietly towards the sounds, increasing in volume and urgency as he neared his village. Screened by a large palm and a safe distance away, he was horrified by the scene in front of him. Men were roped and huddled together in the center of the village. Women sat close by with children and babies clasped to their breasts. Several bodies were scattered across entrances to the huts and at the edge of the forest. The scent of gunpowder, combined with an overwhelming sense of panic and fear, permeated the air. Glazed and unnaturally bright with tears, eyes stared at a chaotic space in disbelief, a nightmare surely, as mothers attempted to croon wailing babies to an impossible silence.

He assessed the scene. The white men had rifles and were pointing them at the villagers. A large black man with tribal markings yelled at the Blacks to be silent, then pointed his firearm at the women. All went quiet except for a few babies until they were offered the comfort of a breast. An old woman came out of the forest suddenly, screaming and running towards the large black man with a scythe. Before reaching him, a shot rang out and the woman collapsed onto her back, an irregular stain of red spread across her chest, a grotesque mortal wound. Henry wanted to run forward and attack these murderers, these slavers, but he had no weapon, only a fish knife in his belt.

The men and women were forced to stand and were roughly pushed forward, shuffling along, restraint as foreign to them as the repressed fury oozing with every reluctant step. Henry thought about his betrothed and felt a terror take hold of him, before he remembered. She would have gone with her mother to her grandmother's village for the wedding preparations the night before. Her grandmother was ill and could not travel; this would likely be the last time she would see her. He prayed this was so and realized he would need to stay alive to warn them of the danger. He prayed she was safe.

There was movement behind him, and looking back, he felt a sharp blow to his head, disorienting him. He was pushed to the ground and held down, hands bound, then forced to his feet and prodded forward. Blows were rained on his back as he walked, his progress hampered by the constant sting of whips against his legs. The smell of smoke reached him, and as he turned his head, he saw flames shooting into the morning sky. He felt another blow as he was ordered to look ahead. The scent of burning leaves, wood smoke and charred bodies carried on the prevailing wind would be his last memory of his homeland and the serenity and freedom of a life he would not know again. He and his fellow countrymen and women started on a march that lasted hours. They finally arrived and were housed in a large stone holding area, earthen floors damp with the pervasive odors of sweat, urine and excrement, where they were branded before being funneled, a few days later, through a narrow stone archway that led down to the beach and the floating prison ahead.

He could not have imagined a worse fate until thrown into a dark, dank hold aboard one of the last illegal slave ships to leave his native Africa. They lay on their backs head-to-head, toe to toe, side by side, bare skin to bare skin, the sickly-sweet odor of fear-laced sweat and the overpowering stench of body fluids oozing from every orifice. He could not imagine a hell more horrific until the boat set sail and the ocean began its relentless assault; currents, wind, and waves in an interminable onslaught, tossing the shackled human cargo against each other. If a knife were to suddenly appear, he was certain not a single occupant of this floating prison would have refused its sharp relief. Every man, woman, mother, father, or child would have gladly gone to the promised land come morning and derived righteous satisfaction imagining the wrath of the slavers deprived of their cache of black gold.

He should have been more aware of his vulnerability. For years, the trade in slavery had been rampant; tribal leaders both inland and near coastal villages had been enslaving their own people black men and women, then selling many to white slavers. Slaves were a profitable business and had been used as currency in Africa for centuries.

His had been a small harbour, certainly not large enough to allow a fully masted ship to set anchor. It was protected by an outer island, uninhabitable due to the dangerous shoals and rip tides that protected its perimeter. Another shiver passed through his body as he remembered an earlier time.

Chapter 9

It had happened during his 'seeking' as a boy. It was an omen; his father had warned him when he had returned home. But he was young and strong, and omens were to him like the stories told of old hags and witches, merely superstitions and meaningless.

'Yo been baptized in dees waters. You remember yo seeking,' his father had chastised him.

How could he forget. Henry had not forgotten his seeking or his baptism. He could not tolerate being confined; claustrophobia was an alien concept to him. But alien or not, it fit.

He had started 'seeking his soul's salvation' as a young teenager with a vision, as was the tradition. (12). His spiritual leader was Mafar, a respected elder. He was required to remove himself from his people, so he decided he would isolate himself on the outer island.

"Wat better test din dat?" he had boasted to his father.

"De woods be safer. How you goin' to speak to Mafar ebry nite when you is off on de island."

"I come back ebry night."

"De tides be strong."

But Henry knew better. There was a way round the far side of the island. He had heard stories. There was even a beach and a sand bar. It would be easy to get ashore and he didn't have to bring any provisions, only water, because he wasn't to eat or sleep while isolated and praying.

"Uh be fine. Uh knows dees waters."

And so, it unfolded. Henry left at dawn, water in a jug at the bottom of the fishing boat and, sailed out of the snug harbour and plied his course to the distant shore of Tukrey island. The sea was calm and the air warm. The morning breeze stiffened as the sun rose on the horizon, revealing a red sky that warned of a change in weather. He should have turned back to shore, but he was halfway to the island and filled with a kind of hubris unusual for him, who often chided his younger siblings to heed the signs of dangerous weather. He tacked into the wind, mindful of staying on course on the leeward side of the island to avoid the shoals. The windward side would be a challenge, but he wasn't afraid.

He tacked back and forth until he had cleared the shoals and continued, confident of his boat and his skills. He felt the first stirrings of anxiety when he navigated into open water, and his boat heeled over with a sudden heavy gust of wind. Holding the rope to stabilize the sail, he stretched his young, lithe body out over the churning sea to act as a counterweight to the tilting motion of the vessel, the sail ballooning in the wind. The current seemed to be moving the boat away from the island and further into the vast expanse of sea. He watched as his refuge grew smaller and realized he needed to rethink his course before he was set adrift at the mercy of the powerful current and gusts. He tacked a few more times with little effect. His only option now was to come about at the first lull in the wind.

As if answering his prayers, the wind stilled. He released the sail, allowing it to luff as he dodged under the boom. The boat was now broadside to the waves and rocking precariously. He quickly positioned himself on the starboard side and tugged on the rope, felt the wind stiffen and watched as the sail ballooned, filling with air again. The boat was now heading towards land. Henry was finally able to exhale as he steadied his hand on the tiller. Ominous clouds, looming overhead, scudded by as the wind returned with renewed force.

He saw the waves curling over the sandbar too late as he tried to tack, to avoid it, but his efforts were in vain. He felt the sudden jarring of the keel beneath him and the listing of his vessel as he was thrown into the roiling waters. The ocean seemed to be pulling him under as he fought against the current, struggling to reach the surface, fighting the urge to breathe as his lungs seemed on the verge of collapse. With a surge of adrenaline and a final upward thrust, he surfaced. Gasping for air and exhausted from the effort, he treaded water for a moment before looking around him. He was horrified to see the mast level with the sea and his boat taking on water. A strong swimmer, he moved with steady strokes to reach the boat and right it. But the current thwarted his efforts, and he was forced to change his course for land. He had never swum in heavy seas and was surprised at how slow his progress was and how much salt water he was swallowing. His stomach lurched and he tasted the bitterness of the bile in his mouth. As he attempted to spit it out, another wave crashed over his head. How much longer would he be able to keep afloat? He glanced back at his swamped boat when something caught his eye. A small barrel was perched atop a cresting wave and travelling rapidly towards him. He dove under the collapsing wall of sea, then surfaced breathless and gasping for air. His shoulder contacted the flotsam as he reached out of the water and grabbed it. He used his last reserves of energy to pull himself onto the barrel and wrap his arms around its sides. He coughed up another mouthful of brine before resting his head on the slats of the makeshift life raft.

His lungs filled with sea air and his nose with the scent of fish as he inhaled deeply. He suddenly realized that his savior was the empty fish barrel from his boat. Another wave crashed over him, and he held on as he was washed over the sandbar and propelled towards the shore of Tukrey island. The sea had calmed here beyond the bar, and he found himself being carried effortlessly by the waves towards land. He struggled to stand in the shallows and, with great effort, was able to push the barrel ahead of him out of the water onto the shore, well above the high tide markings. He stumbled and lay on his back, grateful for the residual, comforting warmth of the sand radiating through his body. Momentarily relieved, he stared upwards at an angry grey sky.

'I must get to shelter before nightfall,' was his final thought as he succumbed to an overwhelming exhaustion.

His eyes jerked open. A crow had landed on him and was pecking at something crawling across his leg. He startled, and the bird took flight, its talons digging into his flesh before it ascended. Remembering the harbinger of bad luck that ravens represented, he shuddered, gooseflesh rising over his body as he pushed himself upright. Instantly, he began to cough, his chest heaving with every gasp until, finally, his stomach emptied its briny contents with spasmodic contractions, sudden and violent. He bent forward, arms binding his abdomen, willing the pain to still. He fell forward onto his knees. His head throbbed as he squinted into the distance at the fading light, the sun making its descent towards the horizon. He realized his vulnerability; his clothes clung to his body and offered no protection from the cold the darkness would bring.

He would need shelter and fire. For a moment panic seized him. How can I make a fire with nothing? He was aware of the tide slipping away, as it washed over his feet, the sand tumbling reluctantly in its wake back to the sea. He looked down at his trembling body and only then did he notice his necessities bag still clinging to his waist by a worn rope.

"Tank you, Jesus," he said and looked skyward as if expecting a celestial response. The sky cleared momentarily, allowing the crescent of a new moon to peek from behind a cloud in the shape of a turtle, a gentle reminder of the favorite meal of his father's. He smiled at the memory. He admired turtles for their tenacity and gentle spirit and had thought how nice it would be to have one as a pet when he was a child. It was whimsy, he knew, even back then. He had often released them from the fishermen's nets before they could be taken and sold. To him, it had been as much a game as a mission. How carefree he had been back then, how mindless in comparison to his life at this moment.

He was aware of an itch and began to scratch his arms, then bent over to ease the irritation on his legs. Sand fleas. He would need to find some

Everlasting plants to treat these, but his most urgent need now was shelter before darkness enveloped the island. He had never realized that the visions of salvation he had imagined experiencing this night would have more to do with near drowning than the spiritual kind he had anticipated.

He walked along the beach, turning inland and climbed, noting rock formations and shallow cave-like indentations. He could hear the high-pitched buzzing of insects coming from the forest beyond as the landscape became more verdant. He gathered some dry brush as he progressed and felt the bite of several large mosquitoes that had found his scent. He realized the forest would be an uncomfortable place for rest, and sleep would not easily come that night. Looking ahead and slightly uphill, he noticed an opening that swallowed a shaft of fading sunlight. He altered his course, climbed the embankment cautiously, and scanned the area, wary of other inhabitants who might not appreciate his intrusion. A bird swooped overhead, and he ducked to avoid an airborne attack. He watched as it settled onto a nest in a nearby tree.

A freshwater stream trickled down the embankment that abutted a cave. Henry knelt beside it and savored the clear, cold liquid. His thirst quenched, he rose and entered the cave slowly, senses alert for any sounds, scents, or sudden movements to indicate animal habitation. He followed its winding path for a few yards before it opened into a spacious area with an unexpectedly smooth floor. It was as if it had been designed for gatherings or living quarters. Scattered, bleached skeletal remains occupied a corner of the space. A narrow, elevated shelf-like structure to the right seemed large enough to allow someone to stretch out on and, at first glance, appeared dry. He ran his hand over it and although slightly damp, it was better than being outside exposed to the elements.

He placed his collected brush on the shelf on top of some dried debris that resembled leaves and pulled his flint from his pouch. After several failed attempts, he had a small fire going and was grateful for the heat, however meager it might seem. He ventured out of his shelter and down to the beach to collect driftwood and whatever kindling he could find. He made his last foray and returned to the cave just as the daylight disappeared and thunder sounded in the distance. Once his fire was well stoked, he lay on the platform, legs pulled to his chest, and watched the play of light and flickering embers, dancing off the walls around him. He looked up and noticed a blackened ceiling- soot, most likely from previous fires. He was not the first visitor to this cave. Some primitive markings were on the walls, crude outlines of a fish and a man. He was reminded of his father and imagined him waiting anxiously for his return and suddenly felt ashamed of his decision not to heed his warning.

Alone and far from home, for the first time in his life, he felt a nauseating malaise, a sense that his perception of security could be distorted, altered without the framework of familiarity, the realization that the confidence he had experienced when he was with his father was false, dependent entirely on his father's presence. He felt foolish; bravery couldn't be taught or learned by observation he realized now. He swallowed the spasms of panic that clutched at his chest and throat.

"Please, God, help me."

His wails echoed off the walls of the cave and reverberated inside his skull. His breaths were rapid and shallow, his heartbeat pounding in his chest; he felt dizzy and closed his eyes. His hands were numb and curled into claws. He remembered listening furtively outside the huts during the birthing rituals, the midwives breathing slowly with the laboring mothers, and the calming effect of the practice. He willed himself to emulate them. Moments later he regained some semblance of control and was able to open his eyes. The trembling in his hands stilled as he opened them slowly.

Bird calls and strange feral sounds, not unlike those of the forest he inhabited on the mainland had stopped; rolling thunder and wind-driven rain now penetrated the silence of the cave. Henry shivered as he stood, adding more brush to the fire, hoping that it would last until first light. An unexpected pressure in his abdomen signaled the need to empty his bladder. Reluctantly, he went to the mouth of the cave, feeling his way along the walls as he progressed. Keeping well back from the opening and the tempest that raged outside his refuge, he began his stream, spraying it in a wide arc in front of him. Hopefully, his scent would deter any predators, and if not, the smell of smoke would ensure his safety. Once inside the cave again, he climbed up on his makeshift bed; the heat had warmed the rocky surface of the stone, and his clothes were losing their dark wetness. He curled into a compact ball with his cold feet near the fire. Sleep did not come as quickly as he had hoped. He thought of Mafar and what, if any, visions he might have during his isolation.

But the only visions that plagued his restless sleep were those of his beloved village and the security of his father's presence. He had no idea how he would survive the night without him.

. . . .

He awoke to find his fire reduced to ashes and a shaft of light penetrating the darkness in a distant corner of the shelter. He rose slowly, his body cold and aching, his legs weak as he followed the light to the entrance of the cave. His outstretched arms welcomed the daylight as he spoke,

"Tanks be to God."

He stared at the horizon, which, from this elevated position, provided him with a panoramic view of the ocean and the sun rising into a cloudless sky over the mainland in the distance. His eyes lowered as he scanned the shore below and noticed a familiar object floating in the shallows near the rocks.

"My boat," he cried out aloud.

He descended the incline cautiously. He didn't need to injure himself now with salvation so close at hand, as he ran along the beach. He recognized the shape of a turtle carved into the side of the bow of his boat. But was it still seaworthy?

He stepped into the water and circled it. The keel was still intact; he was grateful for that. His sail, although a bit tattered, was still whole, and he felt optimistic about its seaworthiness. He dragged the vessel higher onto the beach and noticed a crack in one of the boards in the hull that had allowed water to enter. He tore a section of cloth from the hem of his pants and searched the beach for a piece of driftwood. He didn't have far to look. He used a small knife from his necessities bag and carved out a thin slice of wood from it then extracted a small brown pot from his bag. He scooped out some pine tree resin, applied it liberally to the gap in the hull, and laid the thin slice over it. He did the same to the thin strip of cloth he tore from his pant leg, stuffing it into the gap, effectively sealing it from any further leakage. It was a makeshift repair, and the hull would require a proper sealing when he reached home. It needed drying, but the sun was strong, and high tide wouldn't arrive until midafternoon. With any luck, he would be gone by then.

By midafternoon, the repair was tested and deemed watertight. His fish barrel was loaded into the bow of the boat and as predicted, the rising tide had reached the vessel as he pushed it into deeper water and hauled himself aboard. He still had the sandbar to deal with, but the wind had abated enough to allow the currents to take him parallel to the shore and if cautious he could maneuver through the deepest part of the shoals.

He entered his small harbour just as the sun was setting. He saw a group of people waiting on the shore, waving and shouting, his father among them. He was grateful to be home.

....

The day he had returned home from the island seemed to belong to another lifetime, just as the day he had been captured and shipped across the ocean seemed like it belonged to someone else's life. He had not known a day of freedom until two days ago. He had had scarce time to think of his family and his lost love since he had escaped the mines and could not imagine what they were doing now. He felt weighted down, fearful that they may have suffered a fate like his.

He had jumped off the train two days after he had boarded it. (13). He had been near Savannah and knew he needed to get to water. An old Black fisherman in a leaky bateau agreed to let him fish with him and, in return, would put him ashore at the nearest island. He'd made his way inland in hopes of finding food and perhaps a plantation where he'd heard of blacks owning land and living free. One thing he knew, the air was sweeter here. The saltwater of the sea islands had cleared his head of the oppression of the coal mine and stink of prison, its floors wet and rancid with the piss and excrement from hundreds before him, the sickly acrid stench of death hanging in the air. Sweat poured down his forehead into his eyes, blurring the overgrown path ahead. He kept close to the trees, dripping their lacey moss onto his shoulders as he moved stealthily, mindful of any movements or sounds of human trackers. Thankfully, the shotgun had missed its target, and the dogs he'd anticipated joining the chase had never materialized.

He'd been lucky. He stared into the distance and knew the ocean was close at hand. He'd been grateful for the biscuit he had stolen but was remorseful for the way he had robbed the young mulatto girl of her food. He hoped he would meet her again to ask her forgiveness. He hadn't heard the rumors of a school for freed slaves but wondered; if it was so, could he find work there. He thought about the young girl and was amazed that she had escaped capture. How far had she travelled unaccompanied in a country she had likely never been before? This was no ordinary slave girl. She had been frightened by his sudden appearance, and he recognized her hesitancy even as she warned him to leave, threatening to reveal his presence. She was defiant when addressing him but had distracted the young white girl from entering the shed where he was hiding. She was a mysterious little thing, although one thing seemed apparent- she had a backbone of steel. He had a feeling he would be seeing her again.

Chapter 10

Lucy awoke and peeked out the small window of the shed. Emma had not returned. She had heard a loud commotion before she had fallen asleep, horses neighing and a wagon rumbling along the road. Barking commands drowned out by women's strident pleas and cries in the distance. Where did the horses come from? Have Emma and her family left? Would they return?

She felt uneasy, gnawing in her gut, an anxiety she may have explained as instinctive had she known the word. She understood self-preservation, a skill she had honed diligently during her twelve years in captivity. Did she need to leave now? Was she impulsive? She had heard of the dangers of night travel, but she knew the horrors of enslavement. She slipped out of the shed and looked in the direction the slave had taken. If the Freed Slave school was on St. Helena Island, she would find it. What else could she do?

She walked along the treed path covered in mottled afternoon light and turned towards the house. It appeared deserted; no light was visible in the windows, and the wagon was nowhere to be seen. She heard hoofbeats in the distance that became louder and louder. She moved back into the forest past the shed and climbed a large oak tree draped in Spanish moss. Before long, a group of soldiers in blue uniforms and caps approached the house carrying rifles. They dismounted and tied their horses to the fence posts and began to circle the building, rifles at the ready. Several men climbed the stairs and spread out across the veranda, looking into windows and pounding on doors. Two soldiers opened the front door and entered with rifles primed. She could hear loud noises like breaking glass and overturned furniture, slamming doors, and heavy footfalls on stairs. A few moments later, they reappeared carrying whiskey jugs and laughing with glee.

"No sign of any living thing in there, Captain."

"Men, grab some more gunny sacks from the wagon and collect food, drink, and small valuables. Leave the furnishings, the beds, and the kitchen goods. They will be taken care of when our troops pass through later; we don't have space for them. All spirits must be accounted for, so place them in the crates with the others in the wagon," the Captain ordered as the soldiers returned to the house. He shifted his gaze and lifted his head skyward. A bank of dark clouds was forming in the distance, and a brisk wind was beginning to build into something that heralded something more ominous.

"Let's move quickly, men. There's a storm coming in from the East, and we don't want to risk our gunpowder and supplies getting wet.

Check the pens and any outbuildings that are still standing. Burn any that might hide rebs."

A squeal in the distance was silenced with a sharp report of a musket. Two white soldiers appeared moments later carrying a sow hanging from a sturdy oak bow strung up by its hocks. A loud cheer emanated from the gathered militia.

"Finish up here, men. We'll have a good pig feast once we set up camp by the river. Before long, we'll be back in Port Royal."

A general murmur of agreement, a few 'Yes Sirs,' rippled through the regiment as they moved with renewed energy and the promise of a juicy reward at the end of their foray. Within a short time, the soldiers had vacated the house and with them, all the provisions they could carry, loaded onto their wagons.

Lucy noticed a plume of smoke rising from the woods where she had spent the night in the shed. She hoped it wasn't so, but it seemed the soldiers had likely burned it too. It seemed the only logical explanation. The soldiers continued to move away along the dusty road without a backward glance. Within a few moments, they were gone. Then, blessed silence. She remained in her hiding place until her feet cramped, and her legs began to twitch from inactivity. Satisfied there were no soldiers remaining, she climbed down from her perch and moved towards the shed.

She could feel the heat before the smoke enveloped her, forcing her to step back from the blaze. Her first thought was where she would sleep. Her second thought. What if it spreads? This second problem was the most immediate threat. The vegetation had remained damp from recent heavy rains, but the Spanish moss provided ready fuel for a hungry blaze. She stopped at the stream and realized it separated the shed from the rest of the plantation. The smoke had dissipated somewhat as she forded the brook. The fire was miraculously burning itself out; the bale of hay that had been her bed was visible through the haze and was reduced to a small, charred mound of ash. The soldiers must have set the fire.

Hesitantly, she circled the area, turning her head constantly, alert to any movement that might spell the end of her journey. She moved stealthily towards the plantation house veranda, climbed the stairs and reaching the door, depressed the brass doorknob and tensed as it creaked with the sudden movement. Inside, the destruction she had feared when the Union army had invaded the home had been delayed, likely on the orders of the captain. Tables were overturned; photos and books, including a large leather-bound bible, were strewn across a beautiful woolen carpet. Lucy lifted the bible and scanned the first few pages, grateful for her knowledge of the written word, however limited, gleaned from observing the Massa's children's homeschooling. The first revealed, in beautiful script, a listing of people and dates. Leafing through the tome, a vellum sheet with a map of what appeared to be a house and surrounding grounds with X markings in several spots spilled out and drifted onto the polished pine floorboards. She carefully folded it and placed it in her pocket, uncertain of its meaning, but some unseen hand seemed to be guiding her movements.

She moved into the pantry, praying that it had survived the scourge. Open cupboards had been stripped of most foodstuffs, with doors hanging from their hinges at odd angles while others lay broken on the floor. She stepped forward and tripped over a loose floorboard; as she did, she was reminded of the plantation house where Massa often kept his valuables hidden under the floor, fearing they might be stolen by slaves to raise a rebellion.

House slaves on her plantation talked about money, jewelry, deeds, and documents that were hidden between pages in books, up chimneys, under henhouse nests, in hollows of trees, or buried in fields and behind outhouses. Rumors abounded that when the Union allowed the army to forage for contraband, the soldiers took advantage of the opportunity. They ripped apart houses, outbuildings and slave dwellings, looking for valuables. Families were often left destitute and starving, many fleeing their homes, fearing for their lives. Owners often hid their slaves in secret rooms and passageways, in part because the slaves did not want to be conscripted into the war but also, because the Massas hoped to retrieve them, considered currency, once the army had moved on. (14).

She had witnessed her Massa pulling up floorboards in the kitchen to hide his money after a slave sale. It was to be accessed by the Massa only. She was hoping for food here, but money would be helpful on her journey as well. She looked down at the loose board and had a thought. Why not try? Leaning against the wall in the corner was an iron poker. She wedged it between the planks, levering it slowly until it gave way, then grabbed its end and pulled with all the strength she could muster, until the cavity was exposed.

Lucy sighed heavily as she stared at an empty space. What a silly girl she was. Why would anyone leave a cache of money and goods behind? Wiping her tears from her cheeks with the sleeve of her shirt, she chastised herself for her foolishness. She was about to replace the board when a faint glint of gold caught her eye, reflected in the daylight streaming through the window. She reached in and felt beyond the opening. Her small hand grabbed onto something cold and smooth to touch.

Instinctively, Lucy looked behind her, wary. Confident she was still alone, she tugged gently with her right hand, fearful of breaking it or losing her grip. With her left hand on the floor, she braced herself and let the resistance ease. Still holding the link, she gingerly pulled at it again, and it came away freely with effort. In her hand was a necklace with a gold cross and a stone, the rich blue of a sky on a cloudless day, inlaid in its center. She put it in her pocket before picking up the poker and removing a few more boards, hoping for more treasure. Darkness was all that greeted her as she peered inside the vacant space and heard the scurrying sound of a small animal, likely a mouse, before it disappeared. She reached in once more, and this time, her fingers glanced over an irregular package of some kind. The sun was moving westward, and any remaining light was swiftly disappearing.

She returned to the sitting room and took an oil lamp, thankfully intact, from its perch on the wall. Opening a drawer in a side table, Lucy retrieved a match from its box. She lit the lamp and carried it into the kitchen, its bright light illuminating the interior. She set the lamp on the floor before angling her head into the opening, thankful for her small frame. The outline of a rectangular package was wedged in the corner.

Her hand grazed it, but she needed just another inch or two to get a firm hold. Afraid to get her head stuck and unable to free herself, she retreated. Once upright, she grabbed the poker and maneuvered it into the hole between the wall and the package, then gently inched it towards her. She repeated this and, after a few unsuccessful attempts, finally grasped it firmly in her right hand.

She removed the hemp tie and unwrapped the ragged leather binding, likely a victim to a hungry mouse, revealing a single sheet of paper. The document was well preserved and had signatures on the bottom and a wax seal. The paper reminded her of the expensive vellum that she had seen in Massa's house. She scanned the document and its signatures; this one looked a lot like one of her Massa's with what possibly could be the names of family members and dates of birth carefully listed. On another paper were columns with what appeared to be names and numbers, likely a slave list.

Disappointed that her efforts had produced so little in the way of food or money, she rewrapped the documents inside the leather bindings. She thought about throwing it back in the hole but hesitated. It could mean death if it was found on her and presumed stolen. Or it could help relatives of these slaves find a family member and perhaps be reunited, like she was hoping. The Union Army was capturing or killing Confederate soldiers, rebels, and civilians; the Massas and their families had run for their lives as they had likely done here at Emma's home. She doubted this place would be standing tomorrow after the soldiers returned. If rumors were to be believed, most of the plantation houses were being burned to the ground on the mainland; even the fields were being razed by the fleeing Southerners, confederate soldiers, and Union armies to prevent opposing forces from using contraband goods to fund the fighting. It wasn't only slaves who would go hungry now. Hesitant, she placed the package on the counter and felt the inner pocket of her skirt where the new necklace sat next to her mother's beaded bracelet, the sole legacy of a woman taken so suddenly and brutally.

Chapter 11

Lucy was tempted to stay in the house until the next morning, but she was afraid. What if the soldiers returned before she awoke? The sun hadn't yet set. And she needed food. She looked around the larder she was standing in, then raised her eyes to the top cupboards. None of those had been opened; maybe the soldiers had been in too much of a hurry to leave after they had found the whiskey. A step stool was leaning against the wall. She moved it and climbed until she could reach the upper door. She saw nothing from where she stood, so she clambered onto the counter and peered in. A single jar of preserved peaches and another one containing what appeared to be applesauce had her mouth watering. Scanning the other cabinets, she found a few stale biscuits and a small bag of grits. She carefully removed the jars one by one and set them down carefully. These would keep her stomach still for a day or two.

She opened the peaches and then searched the drawers before locating a bent spoon. She savored the velvet texture of each crescent, gently biting into its slippery flesh as it glided over her tongue. Its sticky sweetness clung to her fingers as she upended the jar and let the syrupy residue trickle into her gaping mouth. She set the empty container aside and, one by one, diligently sucked the nectar from each of her calloused fingers. Nothing in her memory equaled this delight. She placed the biscuits in her pocket along with the spoon, took the applesauce and grits, and filled a small burlap sack that hung on a nearby hook. She took the leather package from the counter and added it to her trove. She felt strangely energized as the fruity liqueur entered her bloodstream, infusing every cell, each complex structure, hungry for its simple fuel. Her body was vibrating, and inexplicably, Lucy was suddenly possessed by an urgent need to move, to leave this forsaken place, where she was a stranger, uninvited and alone.

She entered the sitting room when a jagged shard of lightning pierced the sky beyond the window and tensed as the rumble of distant thunder echoed overhead. Sheets of rain driven by gale-force winds began slapping at the panes of leaded glass, followed by a heavy thudding noise. Lucy had experienced hail before, but not from the inside of a plantation house. These walls didn't move, and the roof above her remained intact. Her instinctual fear of storms was influenced by the feeble structure of slave homes. Made of rough wooden planks with earthen floors and flimsy shutters on empty windows, they kept in the worst heat of the summer and welcomed the chill of winter. Window glass was a luxury for most. The tabby fireplace and chimney made of crushed seashells, limestone, and mud offered the only relief from the damp and cold. She remembered huddling in a corner, clenching her doll Lady, to her chest, praying for the storm to pass, her body shrouded in a blanket, wondering if she too would be sucked out of the window along with the shutters.

The sudden silence was unexpected. Her hands were still covering her ears, and her eyes squeezed shut to the tempest outside. The wind, rain, hail, and thunder had abated as suddenly as they had appeared. No pails on the floor, no sodden bedclothes to air out, no slats to repair in Emma's fine house. She was disoriented and unsure of herself. She was a stranger in this place, unwelcome, however abandoned it may appear. It was an illusion like the freedom promised her. She was not safe. The sun would be setting soon, and she needed to plan her next move. The effects of her sweet meal were starting to take effect, and she experienced a sudden fatigue. She would need to sleep before heading out on the next leg of her travels. She hesitated.

'Should I go upstairs? Sleep in Emma's bed?'

Most slaves, except for housemaids, had never been allowed to enter any rooms in the Massa's house except the kitchen and the sitting room unless the Massa demanded a task of a more personal nature from one. She shuddered. No one was in the house but her. What did she fear? Lucy thought about it and attributed her hesitation to something more familiar and simpler, a provoking of evil spirits and an ingrained superstition that ill may befall someone in a place where one is not welcome. Hers were a superstitious people. She knew many stories and had seen the effect of Black magic, Hoodoo, Voodoo, Hags, and hexes inflicted on people in her community; often they were visited on slavers and their families in retaliation for an injustice. Vulnerable as she was, she was not about to test its influence now.

The house held a small front room where a settee sat below a leaded window. She had seen it from the pantry, and its location would be an ideal place to rest. She would be alerted and have a clear view of any approaching soldiers. A woolen shawl lay at the foot of her makeshift bed, and she shook it before laying it over her legs that were covered in welts after relentless assaults from sandfleas and mosquitoes in the woods. The itching had subsided. She was still alive, and her stomach was full, another blessing. Her clothes were dirty, and the soles of her shoes worn wafer thin; her toes blackened from days of walking through muddy ground, poked through the leather of the first and only pair of shoes she had been given on her eleventh birthday. Her hair was in knots, and she was unsure when she would be able to bathe again. But she had to keep moving. Closing her eyes, she reflected on the escape. Had it only been a few days? The possibility that she could be on St. Helena soon seemed like an impossible dream. But without her dream, what else did she have? She drifted off into a restless sleep; visions of her mother wove into her dreams.

She woke to the sound of a persistent tap on the window, opening her eyes to an inky darkness and lay motionless. She was positioned so she was not visible from the outside. The tapping continued irregularly until the little girl decided that it was likely not human. She lifted her head and peered outside, careful not to expose herself more than necessary. A broken branch from a palmetto was hitting the window with each gust of wind. Grateful to be alone, she realized that she should get going before sunrise. A clock began to chime; one, two, three, four, five, six, seven, she counted as it rang out and echoed through the house. She doubted she had ever slept this long in her short life.

She rose and hesitated as she folded the shawl. Should she take it? The house would likely be razed by soldiers or vandals and doubtless, everything inside it. A shawl would be the least of the soldiers' concerns. She could return it to Emma if she met her again, she reasoned, along with the necklace she had found. Tying the wrap around her waist, she collected the burlap Croker sack containing the treasures found in the larder.

As she moved towards the front door, she sensed a tremor rising through the aging floorboards, releasing pockets of dust into the atmosphere like a fine mist. The distant but unmistakable sound of horses' hooves on dried earth followed. Soldiers? She panicked.

She ran to the larder and side door. She saw the oak tree she had hidden in the day before. Did she have time to reach it? The report of musket fire followed by many others, stopped her progress. The horses were not slowing, and their riders were not dressed in military garb. Flames flickering in the distance bounced to the rhythm of the riders as they approached and stopped at the bottom of the stairs in front of the verandah.

She ran outside through the back door and, scanning her surroundings, spied the door to the root cellar with broken palmetto limbs scattered over it. She cleared away the branches and lifted the handle, praying it would give. It did. A narrow shaft of light pierced the inky darkness, illuminating the earthen floor below. She struggled to gain a foothold on the ladder's narrow, uneven rungs, fearful of falling into the black abyss. Holding precariously onto its rungs as she descended, she reached up and pulled on the trap door, closing it behind her. She sat on the bottom rung and waited, terrified, expecting to be captured at any moment.

'Be patient,' she chided herself.

The hoofbeats began to fade, and when silence returned, peering out from beneath her refuge, Lucy saw the last of the torches swallowed by the forest.

"Tank you, Jesus," she sighed.

The words were barely spoken when she heard gunfire and saw the flashes of muskets fired by mounted soldiers coming from all directions. She scrambled back down the ladder, pulling the door shut once again. The heavy pounding of boots announced their arrival; she could hear their clumsy footfall as they mounted the stairs onto the verandah before crashing through the door. The sound of breaking furniture and smashing windows echoed through the house and reverberated above her head. Suddenly, it seemed there were more hoofbeats now and the unrelenting reports of gunfire reverberating off every surface inside and outside her refuge. Cries of agony and desperation, prayers that would never be answered, ungodly curses, horses screaming, the pitiful entreaties of dying men, pleas she had heard many times before from slaves, but now in voices strange to her ears. Covering her head with the shawl and placing her hands over her ears, she began to sing softly, "Swing Low Sweet Chariot." The sounds of hoofbeats getting closer penetrated the cellar door as a voice ordered the retreat. The gunfire had stopped. She was too terrified to move, silenced by a more deadly threat.

She felt the heat before she saw the smoke wicking through the floorboards above her. She moved quickly to unbolt the trap door and, slowly raising her head, peered carefully over the edge of the opening. Her eyes adjusted to the early morning light as she stepped upwards into an eerie silence and a new dawn.

Around her, bodies of black and white men lay strewn across the landscape, on the verandah, in the gardens, against fences at the edge of the forest, and on the road. Blood-spattered uniforms, severed limbs, and faces no longer recognizable. The young girl had never seen such horror inflicted on such a scale. She'd heard rumors and stories of the terrors of war but had paid little heed to them. What lay before her matched no nightmare she could have imagined. White and Black soldiers, many just boys lying side by side, the victims of battle, fighting for her freedom was almost impossible to believe. How could this be? But the evidence was before her in grotesque reality.

What surprised her even more was the condition of the men and the clothing they wore as she cautiously approached the slaughter. She had imagined crisp gray or blue uniforms with Confederate or Union insignia, but many looked like a mismatched collection of tattered pants, undershirts, overcoats, and caps, making it difficult to distinguish one side from the other and impossible to declare which side was the victor across the killing field. Coagulated blood clung to open wounds from musket balls, bullets, and bayonets while flies and vultures buzzed and feasted on the dead. She saw something moving across one body and on closer inspection recognized the body vermin, an unfortunate case of poor hygiene until she recognized the same affliction on many of those lying prostrate on the ground. Starvation came to mind as she remembered her community gatherings when newly arrived slaves appeared on the plantation, all skin and bones. It certainly applied to these bodies, and the raw weeping sores told of long days of deprivation, filth, and swamp water fever. (16). She heard voices and realized that she was not alone, and watched as the wounded were loaded onto wagons and taken away. They seemed oblivious to her presence. The house was now consumed by fire. She ran along the trail into the forest, well away from the inferno.

Off to the side of the path, beside a tree, sat a man on a crude stool, staring at the destruction and drawing. He was swift in his movements and beside him, a lantern sat at his side. Surely, the poor light made it impossible to see clearly enough to reproduce the horrors that lay before him. He persisted, and a few moments later, a wagon appeared. Lucy retreated behind a palmetto, but it was too late.

Chapter 12

"Where did you come from?" the artist asked in a strange intonation as he put down his pencil and looked towards the young girl. He placed the drawing in his bag with the rest of his supplies and gestured to the wagon standing nearby.

"Get in. You can't stay here. It isn't safe. The colored militia has a base not far away. You'll be sheltered there."

Before Lucy could argue, he had lifted her and her sack onto the wagon before joining her. They moved forward as she stared backward, too stunned to move. As horrified as she was by the carnage she had witnessed, she would learn much later that more soldiers died from diseases than from battle wounds. Poor as her community of slaves was, it was particular about cleanliness. Slaves tended to their afflictions as diligently as they did their gardens that provided their sustenance. What misfortune had befallen these men? She said a Gullah prayer for the many souls that had so recently perished. She peered over the man's shoulder.

"Wuh yo drawin?"

"I'm an artist. I sketch the battle scenes and send them to a newspaper to print." He pulled a copy of Harpers' Weekly from his bag and handed it to his companion.

"See there. That's one I did last month, not far from here."

"Aint yo 'fraid. So many people dyin' in yer pitur."

"Sometimes. I often ride on horseback with the army. I have been shot at many times. I was there when the war began in Port Royal, at The Big Shoot. You need to be careful. Sneaky secessionists' gangs are bloodthirsty. One day, ten soldiers had to escort me to do my sketches. I don't think the confederates like our pictures much. One of my colleagues was captured by the Virginia cavalry but he persuaded the captain to let him go after he did a portrait of their group of soldiers. People need to know what is happening in the war. I get paid for my drawings. Photographers are of little use on the battlefields. Their wagons get too heavy with equipment and get bogged down and can't move in the mud." He turned a page.

"See that picture? That one is by Winslow Homer. He's a wonderful artist. And that one there, by a man called Thomas Nast." She looked at the images and had to agree, not knowing who they were or how famous they might become. (17)

He explained that the weekly she was looking at was one of two popular war issues out of New York City, Harper's Weekly and Frank Leslie's Illustrated Newspaper, chronicling the civil war, its battles, its encampments, and events.

"How does yor pictures git into a paypah?"

"Those sketches and articles get couriered by horse, train, or ship to the publisher's office where the image is copied onto blocks of wood. Engravers take over, and once they complete their job, the picture is electrotyped and copied onto metal plates for printing. Some of these are printed in a newspaper in London, England," the man continued, seemingly happy and proud to have a captive audience.

The artist reached into his bag and pulled out a corn pipe. He leaned back against the side of the wagon and closed his eyes. Lucy looked at the paper in his lap and stared at his drawing, both awestruck and horrified in its accuracy to reproduce such a spectacle of death and destruction.

An hour later, they had arrived at an encampment. Lucy still had her shawl around her waist, and the artist had draped a rough blanket across her shoulders, an insignia embroidered on it. A black soldier in a blue uniform handed her a cup filled with cloudy water. She eyed it warily before setting it down, untouched. When she raised her eyes to assess her surroundings, she was stunned to see a wide field populated by open-flapped tents and a few roughly built wooden shed-like structures scattered over a large swath of rain-soaked muddy ground. Black soldiers were involved in various pastimes, playing cards, gambling, singing to the plaintiff notes of a solitary harmonica, and polishing their rifles and muskets amid a noisy, confused din. Lucy scratched her right arm feeling a welt erupting at her touch. She shed the blanket, untied the shawl from her waist, and wrapped it around her shoulders. She strained to hear the conversation between the uniformed men standing close by. The artist jumped down from the wagon. He said something to one of the soldiers and then waved goodbye to her.

"Wuh we goin to do wid her, Suh?" a black soldier in a blue buttoned up jacket with a row of arrow shapes on his sleeves., asked another soldier.

A white soldier, wearing a double-breasted coat, appraised the young girl as she sat ramrod straight with her chin raised and head inclined away from their line of vision. The water hadn't been touched.

"Where did you get that water, Soldier?"

"Upstream Suh, beyond de camp."

"Don't trust it. We have five men down with the quickstep' filling up the latrines so all water must be boiled (18). And tell the men to dig new sink pits further away from the stream. The rain is coming again, and we don't need our latrines in our tents. Give her some hardtack and a cup of coffee if we can find any."

"Yes, Suh."

Lucy watched as the black soldier proceeded to a large tent. He returned with a cup of hot liquid and two biscuits she recognized as hardtack.

"Here. De coffee be strong ain hot. De hardtack be all we can spare."

"Tank yo," was all she could manage as she dipped the biscuit into the steaming liquid.

After she finished her ration, she felt the need to relieve herself but didn't need to ask where the latrines were. Several men were standing upright in a line on the far side of the encampment beside a large, forested area. Two were doubled over and vomiting into one pit, while another was squatting over another. The stench of sickness and disease permeated the atmosphere with its putrid odor. The woods beyond the latrines could provide the cover she needed and an escape route out of this hellish place.

"Uh needs tuh pass water, Suh."

The soldier motioned to the site where the two men she had seen them relieving themselves.

"Or you can go to de large oak to de left. You won be boddered."

A shout from the large tent, had the soldier abandoning her as she stepped down from the back of the wagon, crossed the muddy field, and approached the tree as directed. Avoiding the latrines, she paused long enough to consider whether she was being watched. Satisfied she wasn't, she escaped along an overgrown path until she reached a tight copse of trees and untrodden ground. She relieved herself before raising her head, then looked around considering the best route to take on her quest to find the school. She remembered to keep her face to the sun and followed a trail to her left that ran parallel to the tiny stream that fed into the camp. She jumped across at a narrow point and decided to walk in the water to eliminate any tracks should she be followed. Sometime later her feet were numb and her spirit lagging. She needed to rest. And eat. Sitting on a large rock that bordered the stream, she dipped the hardtack from her bag into the water until it softened. Somewhat sated, she realized she had no idea where she would spend the night; she had miles to go and was unsure of which direction to take. There were many paths in this area, perhaps due to the increased presence of soldiers and others taking advantage of the chaos the war had created on these islands. She continued, unaware of time, until she happened upon some wild Purslane, which she ate quickly. (19) A hickory tree nearby provided Lucy with a handful of delicious nuts, some of which she secreted way in her large pockets. She moved along the stream as it widened and, to her delight, happened upon a thatch of wild grape. It was rare to find an untouched area of wild fruit since the war began; obviously, no one had passed this way recently. If her luck continued to hold, she would have a full stomach for the next few days. She hadn't seen a mulberry tree yet but as she got closer to wet lowlands, she hoped she would get to taste her favorite fruit.

Trudging along, Lucy encountered some dense foliage, and as she progressed, felt the sharp bite of mosquitoes on her legs and the inevitable aftermath of persistent itching. Thinking of easing the annoyance, she looked about her for everlasting to apply to her legs. Ahead, growing on the slope beside a small marsh, she recognized the familiar orange flower of the jewelweed (20). Remembering how useful it was to ease itching, more so than everlasting, she picked a few leaves and crushed the stems between her thumbs to release the sap. Within a minute of applying it to her legs, its healing salve had worked its magic, and the itching had disappeared. She sat down in the shade of a pine tree on a bed of pine needles and leaned against its rough bark. When she finally looked up at the sun in its westward path, she realized she had been walking for a long time. In the distance, she could hear the faint susurration of voices, and her senses went on full alert. She hid behind a dense growth of palmettos and waited.

. . . .

"You sure this is the spot, Amos?"

"I ain't sure of nothin' except I'm hungry and parched and tired of walkin' Abe."

"We was told to meet the bluebelly, give em 'em what we got, git our money and git out. If this ain't the place we've wasted two days fer nothin'. So, I'm askin' you agin, you sure brother?"

"The camp's about an hour's walk ahead through this bush. We passed the abandoned slaves' huts a mile or so back. Ah can see the smoke risin' to the east, and right here's the only rock we seen for miles. Ah say we sit a spell an' wait."

The taller man, Amos, removed a flask from his bag, pulled the cork, and tilted his head back. Lucy could see him wiping his sleeve across his mouth before handing the container to his companion.

"Anythin' to eat in dat bag?"

Amos burped loudly and produced a hunk of bread from his sac. He pulled it apart, tore a piece off with his teeth, and passed the remainder to his brother.

"Ah don't want to git caught up in no fightin'. I got hardly any powder left for my musket an' the war aint won yet, even if some say it's over," Abe complained.

'There ain't gonna be no fightin'. Quit yer...." Amos stopped mid-sentence and motioned to a large angel oak, its limbs touching the earth, as both moved cautiously behind a stand of pine, weapons at the ready. The rustling of underbrush, steady footfall, and raspy breathing grew increasingly louder. A man in a long, worn, bluish, grey coat appeared in the small clearing, turned full circle, and gave a low whistle in short bursts. He patted his pocket, then leaned against a pine, seemingly relaxed, if not for the steady thrumming of his right foot. At the sound of the whistle, Amos appeared, his gun aimed at the stranger.

"You got the maps?" the stranger asked as he stood and faced Amos.

"You got the money?"

"Why don't you tell your friend to come out from behind that tree, then we discuss this proper-like."

"Abe. Come on out."

Abe appeared slowly, warily, his eyes trained on the man, who smiled as he approached.

"Get them maps from my bag, Abe," Amos instructed as Abe retrieved the maps and placed them on the ground. The stranger looked down briefly before looking first at Abe and then Amos.

"You've got what you want. Now hand over the money," Amos demanded.

The flash of a silver clasp caught the sunlight as the stranger extracted a pouch from his left pocket and, with a single fluid motion, tossed it. Amos caught it deftly and handed it to Abe, who stood beside him as he checked the contents.

"It's all here, "Abe confirmed.

The three men stared uneasily at one another for a moment, before the brothers nodded and watched the stranger pocket the maps then doff his cap in response, and head back towards the forest.

Another flash of silver appeared in the stranger's right hand. He swiveled and called the brothers by name. They turned as one. Suddenly, a shot rang out. Amos was the first to fall. A stunned Abe stared at the fallen brother at his feet and raised his head in time to feel the second bullet enter his body. The assassin approached the two bodies on the ground, two perfect bullet holes in the middle of their chests.

"Bloody traitors." He spat on the two prostrate figures before he searched their bags for valuables. Finding nothing but a worn shirt, an old blanket, and a pair of threadbare socks, he retrieved his money pouch and turned in the direction of the camp.

Chapter 13

Lucy was rooted to the moist earth, the redolent scent of gunpowder lingering in the still air and enshrouding the bodies. The screech of an owl in the distance broke the silence like a feral eulogy. Why did suffering seem to haunt her like a hag's breath? She would never understand how people could exact such terrible brutality on each other without, seemingly, any feelings of remorse or guilt. The bodies lying on the ground were white, not black, not slaves, but the sentence was rapid. No lynching or lashing. Swift white justice with the same outcome.

She had seen so much suffering in her short life, had been the victim of that same brutality she failed to understand, yet for some reason, clung to a grain of hope that people on St. Helena, where she was headed, would be different. Why she persisted in this fantasy, she didn't understand completely. Her father, even though his suffering had been far greater than hers, had been a dreamer and had suffused her with the will to survive and hopefully, one day, thrive and change her world. Perhaps her mother had had similar dreams. Her father had told her she was smart like her mother and to make good use of her God-given gift, a gift she remained uncertain of, alone in this country, the only land she could relate to on a conscious level. She harbored a repressed urgency, a hunger, to return to the home of her ancestors, her unknown family.

'Dis be de only land uh knows,' she thought.

The stories she'd from her father and aunties before coming to this foreign shore had her wishing to belong to a land where she could be free to speak and be heard, where she could live, have a say in her destiny, be seen and treated as a human, not as an instrument of toil, used and abused at another's hand.

She remembered the day her mother had been taken from her; she had been told she had died after being sold. But Lucy felt her father was not being honest with her. She had heard stories about the 'Weeping time" a few short years before the war started when over 400 slaves had been sold, at the biggest slave auction ever seen, in Savannah, Georgia (21). Families had been torn asunder, children wrenched from their mothers, husbands, and wives sold to the highest bidder, never to see each other again, all to pay off the debts of a ruthless slaver named Butler. Perhaps her mother had escaped. Maybe she was still alive. Maybe she could find her once she settled in St. Helena.

She was unaware of the passage of time and the oppressive heat until she opened her mouth to a tongue that held no moisture as it traced a path across calloused lips, agape and raw. She stood, looking around, aware that she was alone with two dead men. The sun was no longer above her but arcing to the west as she moved through a thicket of low brush towards a faint rushing sound. Kneeling close to the water's edge, she cupped her hands repeatedly as she drank her fill from the cool, fresh stream. She felt the gnawing pangs in her stomach, as she stood and looked around; no hickory trees or wild grapes to harvest here. Back near the copse of trees where the men lay dead, she remembered the food they had shared. Was there more in their bags? Did she dare to look? Would it be sinful to steal a dead man's meal?

She walked cautiously into the small clearing. Flies had begun to swarm the bodies, targeting the bloody wounds coagulating in the afternoon heat. Their bodies lay close together, legs splayed at odd angles, arms limp at their sides, eyes wide open, perhaps reflecting surprise at their sudden demise. One bag, appearing to be made of a worn, faded heavy cloth, was torn and lay under the leg of the larger man. Lucy approached cautiously, holding her breath at the stench emanating from the corpse. Their hair was matted, and their faces bearded and embedded with what appeared to be crumbs. They had not seen a bar of lye, a razor, or a bath in some days. She grabbed a strap that was unencumbered and freed the bag from its moorings. Peering inside, she noticed a clothbound with string and using only her thumb and forefinger, pulled it out onto the flattened earth. She untied the package, and some hardtack with a handful of hickory nuts spilled out. Sniffing the contents and noting no rot or weevils, she put the hardtack in her pocket and moved to the other bag beside the second man. It revealed a few hard candies and a small straw doll with a bow around its waist. Surprised at this unexpected windfall, she placed both items in her sac, and before moving swiftly away, she closed their eyes and said a silent prayer over the two men. She broke a branch in four and placed a loose makeshift cross on each of their chests, an atonement and blessing.

Chapter 14

Miss Linda Townley stood on the pier in New York City, her eyes transfixed on the ship she was about to board. She felt a momentary trepidation seize her as she gazed at the name, The Oriental, in neat lettering, inscribed on the side of the ship at the bow. (22)

"The weather looks fine for sailing," her friend Etta commented brightly as she looked out into the bay.

"Looks can be deceiving," Linda retorted in a clipped voice she regretted as soon as the words were spoken.

Etta quickly turned her head in Linda's direction, momentarily taken aback. Linda was the most optimistic person she had ever met, one of the reasons she had volunteered for the mission going to South Carolina to open the school for freed slaves.

"Didn't you sail as a child with your father? "Etta asked, hoping to remind Linda of a cherished childhood memory and brighten her spirit.

"I did."

"And?"

"Only once."

"Once?"

"Once was enough." Linda hesitated and, for a moment, appeared to be in a trance-like state as she gazed out at the vast expanse of water before continuing.

"It started out as a fine day, just like this. My father was a good sailor, and he loved the sea. I thought it might please him if I learned to sail, too. We had planned a special picnic in a nearby sheltered harbor, and I was happy to be spending time alone with him without the nuisance of my sisters. An hour later, a bay came into view. I remember my father saying it was a lee shore and that we would do well to stay clear of it as a sudden gale had risen out of the east, almost laying the boat flat on its side. I held onto the mast before my father ordered me into the cabin while he turned the boat around and headed into open water. It seemed foolish to be going into a storm instead of seeking the safety of a snug harbor. My father lowered the sails and reefed them, he explained when he joined me later. He had thrown sea anchors into the water which I thought curious at the time.

'To keep the boat stable,' he said while we rode out the storm. I could hear the thunderous sound of hail and rain above my head and the roar of the waves as they washed over the deck. The gale seemed relentless, and just as suddenly as it had started, it passed. Emerging from the shelter of the cabin into a sun-washed sky and sea, I was met by the view of an enormous rainbow arcing over the horizon. I collapsed into my father's arms and cried."

Both women stood quietly as Etta clasped Linda's hand. They both looked straight ahead at the huge ship that sat calmly on the water, crew busily attending to their duties on the decks and in the rigging.

"This ship is a lot larger and looks as if it could easily handle any storm."

"I'm not a child anymore, and I understand risks must be taken. I'm going into the middle of a war, albeit with the support of the Union Army. Like the ocean, there are no guarantees of safe passage, but I must do what I know in my heart must be done."

She had experienced many storms since then, living in Boston, a major fishing port, and had been aware of the toll the sea exacted on many New England fishermen and their families, who derived their livelihood from the ocean. She had been an unusually sensitive young girl, perhaps because she was the youngest of four children and acutely affected by the death of her mother when she was still very young. The move from her birthplace, Pittsburg, to Boston shortly after her mother's passing was another upheaval in her impressionable young life.

Before her, the large double-masted steamer was an imposing vessel. Huge sails and rigging formed crisscrossed patterns above the decking like an unfinished spiderweb. At two hundred and ten feet long, it was an impressive vessel and relatively new, having been launched the year before, in 1861, in Philadelphia. It was built as a transport ship for the Civil War. She watched, captivated, as dockworkers moved slowly but steadily, backs bent under the burden of provisions, back and forth over the worn wooden bleached planks of the pier. Ants came to mind.

"What is the cargo those men are putting on board?' she asked Etta.

"I think it's mostly food for the troops; boxes of hard bread, bushels of oats, hay, guns, and ammunition for the troops, I've heard."

"I hope my trunks are safely on board. The medical supplies and books are essential to my work and yours on St. Helena. We can't be of much use without them."

"I'm sure they'll be fine. And you have so much knowledge about medicine now after your training at the Woman's Medical College, you could improvise with provisions on St. Helena."

"There isn't much of anything on the island. The war has seen to that. Food is scarce, and what is available is allotted to the Union troops.

Farming is almost at a standstill. Dr. Hering won't be there to guide me."

"You'll do just fine, and remember, I'll be coming down in the next month or two to assist with the teaching."

"I know, and I am very grateful for your assistance. I know we can make a difference to the freed slaves. I am very excited to be going. Reverend Dr. Furness is committed to helping us. I don't know where we'd be without him."

"When do you land at Port Royal?"

"In a few days. We may have other stops to make along the way. Once we arrive, we will stay overnight in Beaufort for a day before traveling southeast to Ladies Island and then across a narrow river to St Helena. The island itself is small, only six miles wide and fifteen miles long."

"Have you spoken to Mr. Pearce lately?"

"Just yesterday. He has been very busy assisting with organizing 'The Educational Commission for Freedmen' in Boston, Philadelphia, and New York (22). We won't be the only teachers in South Carolina. I only hope that we will be able to convince the negroes that we can help them. The poor children are exhausted from their work in the fields; the cotton harvesting is said to be terribly tiring. I understand that the living quarters of the slave population are unimaginable. The houses are made of rough boards often with large cracks that allow the weather in, windows without glass, and sand or earth floors. People sleep in bunks or on floors. Little wonder there is so much illness."

"Can that be exaggerated? Although I've heard, there are many outbreaks of fever in the region."

"I know. But I am hopeful we can handle whatever we face with God's help."

....

Linda stood on the dock at Port Royal, a few months later screening her eyes from the bright sunlight waiting for her friend to disembark from the ship. She spotted a large, brimmed straw hat and a strained smile peering out from under its shade.

"Etta, you're finally here."

"I am, thanks be to God, and what a passage it was. I was frightened all would be lost at sea including your friend, and such a tempest. But I remembered your bravery as a child and carried on however weak from distress."

"Give me your hand, and we'll go straight to our quarters. I'll get you settled in with a hot cup of tea and some nourishment so you can regain your strength and composure."

"A little brandy may be required as well."

"I think the captain has some good stout sherry in the dining room."

The two women walked arm in arm along the dock and into the chaotic activity of the main street of Port Royal. Union soldiers and sailors headed in and out of taverns, with fights breaking out and spilling onto the road. Mules pulled wagons weighted down with supplies. Sleek horses pulled carriages transporting finely dressed ladies and gentlemen. Along the roadside, Blacks could be seen pushing carts laden with a variety of goods. The din created by the constant activity of the busy Union-controlled port was unlike anything either woman had experienced before arriving in the South.

"Is it always like this?" asked Etta.

"Unfortunately, yes, but we won't be here long. Once we're off the main street at the inn, you'll find it more peaceful." Captain Smith waved as he approached from the opposite side of the road and escorted the ladies to a hansom waiting to take them to their lodging.

The next week the two women continued preparations for the first lessons at The Oaks Plantation, the site of the government headquarters and Linda's new home on St. Helena Island. It had taken a great deal of work to set up desks and unpack books, slates, and writing utensils, but both women felt they were ready. Etta was excited at the prospect of teaching children who were eager to learn and were no longer enslaved. She imagined bright eyes and the quiet concentration of her new pupils. Linda made the introductions. She would be doing double duty as a doctor and teacher as the need for both was great until further recruits arrived from the north.

. . . .

"Welcome. My name is Miss Townley, and this is Miss Murray. We will be your teachers, and this will be your temporary school quarters until a new school can be built close by. You will be getting slates and books for reading, writing, and arithmetic. Please stay in your seats until dismissed."

The first day of school was promising to be a challenging one for both teacher and student, as children stood and began milling about the classroom and did not appear to be listening to what was being said. The women had been warned of the challenges facing children who had never been confined to a desk and chair. They found it difficult to concentrate on anything, and it was exhibited in their restless nature. Most were polite, but their language was difficult to understand. Some thought it was a sign of a weak mind, but the doctor felt it was a language all its own, a strange mixture of French Creole, English, and an African tongue.

Black men and women would sometimes attend classes, too, later in the day, eager to learn to read and write; after the war, it would become common as their thirst for knowledge grew after centuries of repression. Both teacher and doctor, recognized the intelligence of their skilled artisans, blacksmiths, woodworkers, carpenters, masons, seamstresses, and midwives. They were essential not only to the day-to-day operation of the plantations but also an invaluable source of knowledge to the masses about every aspect of crop cultivation, animal husbandry, disease, and weather.

Linda understood from Mr. Pearce, one of the first enlisted men to serve in the war, that the slaves had their own caste system. At the top were the black drivers, similar to white overseers, then the skilled laborers and artisans, carpenters, smiths, masons, woodworkers, and engravers. In the lower ranks were seamstresses, gardeners, cooks, house, and ladies' maids. At the bottom of the scale were the field hands; planting, hoeing, weeding and harvesting crops and any other task that required a strong back and constitution. (22). Young children were often included in this group, whose small hands were ideal for picking vegetables, fruit, and cotton. Slaves were often allotted a plot of land to cultivate for their own use after they had completed the daily tasks of the plantation.

Their medicine men, women, and root doctors had extensive knowledge of herbal medicine and treatment of common ailments prevalent in the low country. During the hot, humid environment at the peak of the growing season, the slaves' medicine had relieved many a planter's family suffering from heat rash, sunburn, stomach ailments, snakebite, wounds, and fevers. In the South, poverty was the norm for most whites, slaves, and free blacks alike, and expert medical care was unavailable to most. Black midwives often delivered babies of both races.

Linda noticed Little Mary one morning with her head on her desk, crying uncontrollably.

"What's the matter, Mary?" the doctor asked as she knelt beside the little girl.

"My papa git de feber. Eh be real sick," she blurted between sobs.

"Is anyone with him."

"My Mama. But she needs ta wuk in de fields."

"Would you like me to visit them? I have some medicine that would help."

"De root doctor be der."

Linda explained the situation to Etta and left the classroom with Mary in tow. She retrieved her medical bag and readied the wagon for the journey to the black encampment two miles up the road. She was anxious, knowing that many Blacks were wary of White Man medicine and may not appreciate any assistance from her.

The slave cabin that housed Mary and her extended family was like many others in the area. It was crudely built with wooden slats on the outside and a thatched roof. Wooden shutters on the windows hung open, and one was hanging on by a single metal hinge. Inside, a fireplace made of tabby- a cement-like mixture of sand, crushed shells, and limestone- took center stage in the middle of the structure. The pungent aroma of okra and fish stew rose from a cast iron pot hung from a hook in the hearth. Rough wooden slats covered the floor, an extravagance here, as most slave cabins used sand or compacted earth. The patient lay on the bottom bunk, and from where the doctor stood, she felt certain it was malaria that afflicted him. Numerous bites covered his body, some oozing a clear fluid. She asked Mary's father about fever, chills, nausea, and sweating, and all answers were affirmative. He had been sick for two weeks and was desperate to get well.

"Can I look at you, Sir?" asked Linda.

He nodded weakly as the doctor did a quick assessment.

"Would you like to have some medicine to get better?"

The man nodded again.

"I'll give you some quinine medicine, and you will feel better soon. I will return tomorrow to check on you."

Mary whispered something in her father's ear, and he swallowed the liquid without hesitation. He looked towards the doctor and nodded in appreciation. Linda noticed a beautiful carving of a bird sitting on a crate beside the bed where a pocket knife and a few pieces of wood lay.

"Did your father make that?"

"Yessum."

"It is beautiful."

When the doctor returned the next day, her patient was sitting up in bed and eating some clear soup. She checked for fever and asked about headaches. Both had improved. She presented Mary with more medicine to give her papa with instructions. Mary's mother looked on from the other side of the room. As Linda started to leave, Mary rushed to her side and placed something smooth in her hand. It was the beautiful carving of the bird she had seen yesterday.

"From my papa," said Mary.

"Thank you. I will treasure it." Linda smiled at her patient before she left the cabin, impressed by the skilled hands of the Gullah man.

Linda realized that not all slaves were immune to tropical diseases, as many plantation owners believed at the time. The doctor estimated that many of the slaves she treated died from mosquito-borne illnesses like malaria and yellow fever in the subtropical climate of the Deep South. The symptoms often recur after periods of remission following treatment. Most were not as fortunate as Mary's father to get proper medical attention and survive. She would have to keep an eye on her students and their families, especially at the height of the summer when malaria and yellow fever were most prevalent.

. . . .

The first students were taught at the Oaks Plantation in May of 1862, but in September of the same year, a new school was opened in the Brick Church, close by, where eighty students were enrolled. Linda and Etta remained both surprised and disturbed by the lack of attention their new pupils paid to their studies. They were diligent in reminding students to sit and concentrate on their lessons, but many continued the same behavior they had observed when the first school opened. Linda wrote to Dr. Hering.

"It was quite disturbing how the students carried on. In the middle of an English lesson, children would stand, curtsy, then walk off to the berry patches in neighboring fields only to return an hour later and curtsy again before resuming their seats. Other times, they would put their heads down on their desks and sleep or talk loudly over the teacher's voice. They were very difficult to understand, and I'm afraid they found my speech confusing as well. At the end of morning's lessons, I was exhausted.' (22)

"Miss Townley, I urge you strongly to return north. The current outbreak of smallpox is too great a risk for you and Miss Murray to handle on your own with limited resources, supplies, and the like. It is a large and needy population, of which I speak. We cannot guarantee your safety midst the negroes and the harsh conditions of the climate and surroundings," a union captain and friend advised Linda and Etta.

"I appreciate your concern, but we did not come here expecting to leave at the first sign of difficulty. The contagion is under control now, and I understand the Freedmen's Association will be sending more teachers to help us with our work. We need to be here to continue our teaching and ministering to the poor people who live here and are suffering. My medical knowledge is a great help."

Linda was aware of the many dangers that she and other teachers faced on St. Helena and neighboring islands, with the war being fought on many fronts, and reports of battles and skirmishes between Union soldiers and Rebels. Now was not the time to be fearful; the children and their families needed them more than ever before. She used much of her own salary to supplement the costs of medicines and supplies desperately needed, for the freed slaves.

Chapter 15

Carried on the wind was the familiar peaty scent of decomposing vegetation, and Lucy knew to stay well back from the marsh's boggy edge. A river appeared as a thin thread weaving its torturous path through the tall golden-hued spartina grasses in the distance. The tide was out; snowy egrets and blue herons plunged their long bills into the exposed grey pluff of the marsh bed before the rising tide submerged their meal of hermit crabs and shrimp. Swooping Sea sparrows and wrens snatched mosquitoes and midges in midflight, returning to tend to their clutch of eggs in nests, cleverly disguised in the grasses and vegetation of the saltwater marsh.

Across the channel, an island was visible. She squinted in the bright sunshine and guessed it was situated in the east as the sun moved westward behind her. How many islands lay between here and St. Helena? Could she navigate the waters that separated her from the refuge she sought? She traced a path along the marsh's perimeter, treading softly and alert to any sounds that might signify danger or an unwelcome confinement. She knew she needed to get to the opposite shore but was uncertain how that could be achieved. She edged closer to the river bed, removed her shoe, and pressed her right foot into the warm grey clay. Pulling back, the dense muck resisted her persistent efforts until her foot was freed with a loud pop. Walking across was not an option, she realized, and needed to wait until the water returned.

She sheltered in a thicket of palmettos and white pines bordering an elevated area of scrub grass and pine needles. It offered a protected view of the water and provided welcome shelter from the wind and sun. She wondered if this were a spot used by locals as it would make a perfect resting place. She stood and wandered down the opposite side of the incline and came upon a firepit circled by rocks with charred wood and ashes at its center. It gave off no heat that she could detect, and on closer inspection, irregular shapes and charred bones scattered about; squirrels and rabbits came to mind. They had been abundant before the war but scarcer now. Everything was.

She wandered a little further into the forest and inhaled the sweet fragrance of the wild paw-paw tree, a favorite of the slaves on her plantation. Hanging precariously close to the ground, a duet of long pale green fruit clung tenuously to a bifurcated limb. Gripping the branch, she removed both and placed them gently on the ground. She retrieved the spoon from her pocket and, with its edge, cut along the spine of one. Juice oozed from the incision until the skin was flayed and the fibrous orange hued fruit exposed. She scraped out and discarded the small toxic brown seeds; many people had become ill with stomach and bowel ailments after eating these. The delicious syrup was soon running over her chin and onto the earth below as she leaned over to avoid soiling her clothes. The fruit was soon dispatched. Appetite satisfied, she gathered the sticky remains and carried them to the marsh. Scraps of tasty food would attract the attention of animals and humans, dangers she had had enough of in the last few days.

Approaching the river, she heard voices in the distance and retreated behind a giant stooped river oak, its branches draping lacy moss and skimming the tops of the reeds that reached up to meet it. A small blue boat was visible on the shore, and a loud exchange was carried over the marsh.

"We'll leave it on shore tied to that tree. At ten, when the Rebs are sleepin', we'll come back and cross over to get the moonshine. Billy said he'd meet us at Ladies Island and help us load. We'll be done before low tide, just like last time."

"You set a better price this time?"

"Same as before. We split the money fifty-fifty."

"He shorted us last time. We take all the risks of crossing the river at night, and he takes half. We shoulda asked for more."

"You ask em. I aint doin' it. I rather git half of sumpin' than a fanny full of buckshot. You don't like it; I'll find someone else."

"Okay, Jeb, I'll go with ya. But I don't like it."

"Me neither. But I gotta face the facts, and the facts is that I'm broke and ain't got no other employ. Unless you have a grand plan you ain't sharin'."

"Fair 'nuff. Let's tie her up under that big oak near those palmettos and cover the oars with scrub brush. I sure as hell don't want no surprises when we come back."

It seemed like ages before the marsh was silent again. Lucy hadn't moved, and her legs were cold and cramping from sitting on the hard ground. She could barely discern the blue bow of the boat, and had yet to decide what to do.

'So dat be Ladies' Islan,' she whispered, staring across the expanse of water. Herons, pelicans, and egrets had taken flight as the tide slowly eased itself into the valleys and spaces between the grasses, covering the rich seafood that a short hour ago had provided nourishment for the shorebirds.

She filled her sack with as many paw-paws as she could carry and made her way towards the location of the boat. The path was thick with palmettos and low brush, forcing her to pick her way carefully en route to her destination. The boat was visible under some large branches, but the oars took more time to locate. Pleased with her discoveries, she chose a spot to rest within sight of her escape vessel. Her plan was twofold: Get the boat into the water and row to Ladies Island with the rising tide after dark.

She had no idea if her plan would work.

Chapter 16

Henry had been wandering for days in the woods, sleeping in abandoned cabins and huts, avoiding Union soldiers, rebels, and slaves like himself. If caught, he would surely be re-enslaved and returned to a hell he had no intention of revisiting. He enjoyed his freedom, such as it was, but food was a scarce commodity. Most plantations, once abundant with crops of cotton, rice, corn, okra, yams, and other root vegetables, had been abandoned or razed by the Massas and Confederate soldiers to prevent the enemy from using them for their own purposes. He'd heard that some freed slaves, those who hadn't been killed by their owners as they abandoned their lands, had taken over and were now farming plantation land for themselves. His mouth watered as he dreamed of corn fritters and hushpuppies; wild berries and hickory nuts did little to still the constant rumblings of his stomach.

He had yet to pass a plantation with slaves in control and had kept his distance whenever he approached a clearing. It was early morning, and the dew on the bracken covered path soaked into the calloused skin on the soles of his feet, sending a chill up his spine. A brisk wind out of the east carried a rhythmic beat, faint but persistent, and increased in volume as his ears to lead him to its source. Overstepping the sharp curved spines of the saw palmetto at his feet, he scrambled up a spreading oak. He was able to stand on its wide branch where it met the trunk. Outlined in the distance was a modest whitewashed rectangular structure supporting an aging roof with several shingles missing. Carried on a gentle breeze, a faint but familiar melody rose to his ears. Closing his eyes, his mind travelled to a distant past, a distant land, a lost family as Henry joined the plaintive chorus of 'Michael Row Your Boat Ashore'. Sitting in a small clearing in the middle of a foreign land, he was overcome with a profound longing at the familiar refrain sung by parishioners in that house of God. He realized the faith he had lost, had at last found him.

He watched from his perch until the music stopped, and the congregation started to file out into the bright sunshine and crisp morning air. A long wooden table resembling an old door supported by two sawhorses was erected beside the building, a colorful tablecloth lay on top as women placed baskets laden with food across its length. Henry could smell the aroma of fried okra and hush puppies as he approached cautiously from the opposite side of the building. He paused to consider his next step when he felt a hand on the back of his neck.

"Wuh yo doin' heah?"

The voice was distinctively Gullah, and Henry was unsure how to respond. He did not move.

"Hungry, is all."

"Weh yo from?"

"Georgia."

"Uh had a son took fo de war. Weh yo fambly to?"

"All daid now. I aint got nobody."

"Yo can eat but den yo gots to go. Uh dun wan no trouble."

"Uh jus needs some food."

"Follow me but dun talk to no wimmin or chilluns."

The man removed his hand and called out to a large Black woman with a colorful apron and head scarf who looked up with her head tilted to one side, questioning. The man motioned, eating with his hands, and the woman nodded. A minute later Henry had a plate of fried okra, biscuits, and Gullah rice on a chipped China plate with some hobo bread wrapped in an old cloth.

"Tank yo," Henry bowed his head. The meal was finished in less than five minutes, and the hobo bread was tucked safely into the traveler's pocket.

Henry stood, hoping to be offered a place for the night, but the man indicated that it was time to leave as he pointed to the path behind the praise house. Henry thanked him again and left, his belly full for the first time in weeks. The noon sun was beating down on his bare head; he needed to find a place where he could settle for more than a day, a place he could call home before he was taken again. He turned his head toward the man who had fed him.

"Yo knows de place called St. Helena. Uh hears yo can fine work der."

"Go East. Yo gots tuh cross de river at de high tide. Watch fer rebels. Dangerous times we be in."

"Much obliged." Henry tipped an imaginary hat and headed off on the path. How to get there, he did not know.

Chapter 17

Silhouetted by fading sunlight, a trio of pelicans swept across the rising waters of the grassy marsh as Lucy crept towards her evening rendezvous. The wind was freshening in the west; fluffy white and gray clouds, like dampened cotton, ballooned over the gilded horizon, promising changing weather. The young girl held tight to the ragged hem of her skirt as she stepped carefully over the thick thatch of ground cover encroaching on the path leading to the shore. She had hoped for a sandy entry, but like so many of her wishes, that dream, too, had disappeared with the tide, leaving a rocky shingle beneath her feet. The rising water, a necessity to traverse the river, was a mixed blessing. Getting wet was the least of her problems. Drowning was her greatest fear.

Under a thicket of brush between twin oaks and palmettos, Lucy spotted a slash of white and, beneath it, an aging hull, its fading teal paint, a hapless victim of the ravages of the saltwater marshes. It appeared larger and longer than she had originally estimated. It occurred to her that moving it might prove to be a bigger challenge than she'd anticipated, and maneuvering it any distance, a formidable one. Lifting the branches for a better look, she leaned over as a briny odor wafted up. Ropes curled in a neat circle, and a small bailing bucket rested in the bow. What appeared to be a large brown bundle smelling of linseed oil and wax lay folded beside them. Its texture reminded her of a raincoat the Massa had worn in foul weather. A rough plank spanned the width near the middle, and the stern was squared off, unlike its pointed bow. Identical prongs were fixed on the leading edge of each side of the boat. She looked for an oar and, finding none, remembered that the men had hidden those too.

Darkness was rapidly descending on the marsh. She scanned the area nearby and noticed fresh-cut palm leaves lying at unnatural angles opposite the boat. She lifted them carefully, avoiding their sharp points, revealing a pair of oars. All that was left now was to place them in the boat and head across the river.

Luckily, the boat rested near the shore, the water now lapping against the bow. She lifted the oars one by one and laid them in the vessel resting against the stern. She placed both hands on the boat and tried to push the vessel into the river, but it resisted her efforts. Using her body as leverage, she turned her back to the boat, dug her heels into the boggy earth, and leaned her weight against its solid mass. The boat moved a little, but progress was slow; she fell backward, landing on her back, her head resting on the muddy turf, her eyes now focused on a darkening sky and the promise of a full moon.

A rustle of branches and a scurry underfoot immobilized Lucy, as she looked for its source. Fear morphed into terror as the footsteps became more pronounced and signaled something heavier and more ominous approaching. As the darkness descended with nowhere to hide and less time to think, she jumped into the boat with her sack, found the bundle, covered her body with it, and prayed.

Time seemed to slow as Lucy heard a muffled grunt and heavy breathing, a lurching forward unsteadily until she felt the boat rocking to the smooth rhythm of water slapping against the hull. She heard another grunting effort, wood knocking against wood, and what was most likely oars being inserted into their locks. She could sense the boat's movement and the splashing of water, the oars creaking, rubbing against metal, as they progressed across the water. The girl remained immobile, barely breathing, wondering how long before she would be discovered. Suddenly, shouting erupted, carried over the water, close enough to hear the desperate yells of men ashore.

"Get back here with that boat. You'll hang for this if we don't kill ya first."

Gunfire filled the air with ear-shattering reports. There was a momentary pause in the attack before it started again, and Lucy could feel the boat being propelled forward, its progress seemingly unhindered by the shoreline assault. The gunfire continued as the boat moved through the river towards what the young girl hoped was the distant shore. Minutes passed as the sounds of muskets faded before she dared to breathe again. How long would it take to reach landfall? Where will I go when I get there?

Where is this water coming from?

She felt dampness under her feet, seeping into the boat and steadily rising. Unsure what to do, she hesitated. The boat was still moving, so it must be afloat, but for how much longer? She could hear the heavy breathing of the sailor and wondered if he had noticed the water intrusion into his vessel. Until he stopped rowing, she would remain hidden, and terrified.

Her feet were submerged as the water level increased and inched its way up to her ankles. She felt the boat slow down, before it abruptly stopped. She felt a pronounced rocking to one side, followed by a splash. The water around her feet was rapidly rising. She couldn't wait much longer. After a few anxious moments, she lifted the cover and peeked outside. The anonymous sailor had disappeared, and most likely swam to shore. She peered over the bow of the boat and saw a dark figure disappearing into the woods. The vessel was taking on water from several holes in the hull where the rifles had found their mark. She realized that she was as vulnerable to sinking as the boat unless she could make it to land. She estimated the distance to shore, but in the darkness, it was difficult to know for certain. Was the water shallow in this area? She was not willing to plant her feet on the boggy riverbed or worse, sink to the bottom.

What to do?

She looked at the oars. If she could tie those together, she might be able to fashion a crude raft to get ashore. Using the rope, she quickly intertwined it between the oars, tying it off tightly. The thought occurred to her that it was a bit like making sweet grass baskets. Then another idea struck her- place the makeshift tarp on top. Praying It wasn't far to shore and thinking should it sink a bit, she would still be protected from the pluff of the riverbed and perhaps stay drier with the cover beneath her. For security, she tied one end of the rope to the boat and lowered the makeshift raft gently overboard.

It floated!

The boat was almost level with the waterline as she eased herself over the side and lay her body across her floatation device. She gasped as the cool water submerged her legs but determined; she started to move her arms through the water in awkward but determined strokes. The land seemed farther away than she had calculated. As she moved forward, her legs sank deeper below the surface. She attempted to reposition herself but to no avail; her feet found the shallow bottom first, and she was surprised to find sand beneath them. Standing in the water, barely touching her thighs, she was overwhelmed with relief.

She had survived the crossing! She salvaged the brown tarp, then pushed the makeshift raft back into the water and watched as it drifted away into the darkness. She could see the boat disappear below the surface; her makeshift raft remained afloat like an eerie watery grave marker. She sat on the tarp, shivering as much from her soaked and dripping clothing as her recollection of another watery nightmare.

....

She remembered her baptism and her anxiety at the thought of being submerged. She had survived her 'seeking,' a test before being accepted into her Methodist congregation; her isolation from the rest of her family in the woods had been difficult but short-lived. There was no time on the plantation for prolonged meditation or contemplation. She was a quick study of the required Catechism. The baptism itself was held at ebb tide when the sins of the converts would be washed away on the outgoing waters. At the creek, as the bishop submerged her in the cold dark water, her eyes remained open, breathless in a senseless panic of impending death, choking on the bitter water before being lifted free of that horror (23).

The 'Shout' was the final part of the prayer meeting after the baptism, where the congregation joined in with singing and shouting, a boisterous and joyous form of worship. Lucy was a reluctant celebrant as a circle-ring dance followed once the floor of the praise house was cleared of benches. She was welcomed as a new member of the church, her salvation ensured. That was a small comfort to the young penitent whose fear of being submerged had remained with her ever since.

Other memories rose close to the surface of her conscious mind; litters of kittens tied in sacks, weighted down, and thrown into the river near her plantation. She prayed for their tiny souls, wanting to save them, knowing she couldn't. Not only animals suffered that fate. She had seen more than one slave drowned in the same river. Watery deaths seemed a recurrent theme in the lives of slaves. Stories resurfaced in her mind, of harrowing journeys to the Americas aboard stinking ships, shackled and packed like rows of wood in airless disease-ridden hulls, often tossed into the churning waters of the ocean, when disease, food, or water shortages, made the slaves' survival redundant.

With so many painful memories, she could only hope that St. Helena would provide a safe refuge from those horrors.

Chapter 18

Lucy climbed a nearby tree and looked down from her elevated roost in the ancient pendulous Angel Oak, its thick foliage an effective screen; she doubted anyone looking skyward would detect her presence on this black night, with the moon hidden behind a thick cloud cover. The war effort had effectively cleared this area of habitation, both human and feral; a subtlety often lost on the islanders, who had diverted their energies towards their own survival and not that of the local wildlife. She could not stay up here much longer; the night had cooled, and the biting insects had found her an easy mark. She climbed down cautiously. She needed all four limbs functional to reach her goal.

Moving slowly through a large clearing, she felt the earth soften beneath her feet and the aroma of peaty earth, decomposing vegetation, and the fragrance of Jessamine filling the air. A sliver of the full moon appeared for a moment and reflected off a pond as she stepped back before it disappeared again. Across the watery expanse, a collection of grasses, dead limbs, and debris formed a silhouette of a floating island. An alligator nest, most likely. A large cypress knelt behind it, paying silent homage to this king of the south. A skink scampered across her path; her larger relative was likely basking somewhere nearby. She had no intention of getting closer; a row of red cedar shielded her from the sloping bank as she circled to her left and the forest beyond.

A path, overgrown but obviously an intentional route, wound through the forest that thinned out as she progressed, leaving a wide clearing. There remained a few young magnolias, loblolly pines, and hickory trees, but large stumps appeared at regular intervals. She bent down and pulled a branch from a small sapling nearby and examined it. Pine. The trees had been felled recently for building, for what exact purpose she was unsure. She understood the effort required to build even a small slave cabin. The Union soldiers needed wood for fire, wagons, and field offices. If the rumors were true and slaves had taken over abandoned plantations, even those burned to the ground, could they be building new homes for themselves?

Color, age, and gender were working against her, but she was determined to push ahead regardless of the challenges that surely awaited her. A freed slave was a free man or woman, and if land was available for the taking, why not take a piece for herself? Lucy was not naïve but wanted to believe the rumors that a freed slave was as entitled as any other. The only variable was money. She wasn't wrong in her belief.

....

She had seen the Black women in the market selling their fruits, vegetables, jams, jellies, chicken, eggs, and pork, not realizing that they had been free long before emancipation ever found its way to South Carolina. She had heard that property was often passed down from mother to daughter and granddaughter through matriarchy lines and hoped one day she could do the same.

Stumbling through the forest blindly, she felt the sting of nettles, wild rose bushes, and the sharp points of palmettos but there was no time to worry about those irritations now. A structure appeared out of the darkness ahead. She approached cautiously and listened at a safe distance for any activity. Except for the crickets, frogs, and cicadas, she could detect no ominous sounds. Pushing through some dense brush, she reached the windowless side, clad in pine boards, and paused.

She felt a sudden chill, the presence of some unseen spirit. She hesitated before approaching the slave house, wary of what or who might lurk inside. She circled the building cautiously, until a persistent tapping stopped her progress.

Hanging precariously from a single hinge, a shutter knocked against the rough boards of the cabin wall to the rhythm of the prevailing wind. Lucy crept forward slowly and peeked through an unglazed frame into an inky darkness. Moving around the structure, she lifted the crude wooden latch of the cabin door and pulled; its creaking protest echoed into the forest. Molly froze, barely breathing but sensing no imminent danger, and entered the dwelling,

The pungent smell of sweat, vomit, and ammonia comingled as she covered her nose and mouth, suppressing a nauseous, gagging reflex. Feeling around the limited space as her eyes adjusted to the darkness, she located an old wooden chair and a small table in one corner and opposite it, the shape of a narrow bed under the pane-less window. A breeze wafted across the room as she moved to the corner; succumbing to a sudden vertigo, she lowered herself onto the edge of the sagging bed frame. The young girl could feel the stitching of the embossed quilt, imagining the large, calloused black hands that had painstakingly created the delicate designs. Lucy felt an unexpected heat from beneath her searching hands; startled, she rose quickly as a skeletal hand grabbed hers.

"Help me."

The raspy whisper emanated from darkness as the grip tightened.

"Water, please."

Fighting a growing terror, she extracted her hand, lifting each finger in succession before placing it on the stranger's abdomen. She stood and moved quickly across the space towards the table, feeling her way with outstretched arms until her legs bumped against a wooden leg. She scoured its surface and found a candle stick in its holder, but sadly no matches. She circled the table and located the knob of a primitive drawer. Inside, her fingers traced the outline of a small box, and as she shook it, a rustling sound confirmed its contents. It was dry, a blessing. She placed the candle near the center of the table and struck the flint. A bright flame filled the darkness as the wick caught. Lifting it to survey her surroundings, she was dismayed to see that there was little else but the table, a lone chair, and a bed. A wooden box sat upturned by the bedside where a metal cup lay askew. The young girl's eyes focused on the other occupant of the space and gasped.

In the dim light, it was difficult to determine the man's age, given the toll whatever illness had inflicted on his body. He looked familiar, but that seemed impossible. The quilt covered his body, leaving only his face and arms exposed; on closer inspection, no pus-filled skin eruptions, thankfully, but a number of bites were raised and crusted over. She had seen many cases of malaria and yellow fever with similarly infected bites. Smallpox, too, was common in both the slave and white populations on the plantations; doctors, nurses, and medicine men and women had attended the victims, sometimes succumbing to the diseases themselves.

Looking after a white man was an unexpected and dangerous situation for her to be in. She had no medicine to treat him, regardless of whatever disease he suffered from. She would do what she could to help: fill the cup with water, put it at the bedside, and escape to a safer haven. She needed to quench her thirst as well, realizing she had not had anything to drink since arriving on the island. Someone would surely return to tend to this man. She would be long gone before that happened.

The patient remained motionless as she opened the door and stepped outside. Thankful for the moonlight that had reappeared, Lucy returned to the pond she had passed nearby, hoping to find a stream feeding it. The loud chorus of cicadas and frogs filled the night air as she stumbled along a scrub path until she reached the pond. There did not appear to be a stream, so she moved on until the burned skeleton of what must have been an old plantation house, appeared through a break in the trees. Was it abandoned? Surely, no human could find refuge there. To the right of the ruins, a raised circular form was visible, perhaps a well. Her old plantation had had one, with a little roof over it and enclosed with latticework to keep animals out. She approached cautiously and was relieved to see that it was indeed covered and the wooden bucket, lying on the ground beside it, was still attached by a sturdy rope; the fire had not reached it. She lowered it easily from years of habit and drank her fill, savoring its crisp, cold relief even as water trailed down the front of her blouse. She filled the metal cup and looked about. She could smell the sweet scent of sage, and her nose guided her to the patch close to the well. The leaves freed easily from their stalk as Lucy filled her pockets with the aromatic cache.

The medicine woman had given sage tea to her patients to treat fevers and stomach illnesses. Perhaps they would help even if she had no proper means of making tea. Perhaps cold steeping would provide some relief. Walking back along the path, voices sounded in the distance. She crouched behind a large oak and waited.

. . . .

"He might be in there. Look, there's light inside."

"I ain't goin in. Might be the pox."

"We were told to find him, and if he's still alive to make sure he's safe and got water and biscuits. If he's dead, we got to bring him back."

"Well, you go in then. I'll wait here 'til you say it's clear."

The door creaked, and the man stepped into the darkness. A minute later, he reappeared on the doorstep.

"It's him. He's alive. Let's move on. There's a storm brewing. We'll come back tomorrow to check on him."

"Okay. We done our bit. Let's go. No need to git the pox ourselves."

His friend's hands were shaking as he replaced the latch, and a moment later the pair had disappeared into the darkness.

The voices dissipated in the distance, along with the sound of retreating hoofbeats. Waiting until all was quiet, Lucy approached the shack, lifted the latch, and stepped inside. The soldiers had been dressed in uniforms similar to the ones worn by the men who had brought her to their camp. Union soldiers, she guessed. Why had they left so quickly? Had they not seen the candle? It was obvious from the condition of the patient that it was impossible for him to sit, let alone walk across a room and light a candle. She placed the cup of water on the table and removed the sage from her pocket. She looked to see if they had left water or food and noticed two biscuits and a flask at the bedside. Ignoring them, she crushed the leaves with the spoon from her pocket and added them to the water. She held the cup above the candle, hoping to heat the tea. It seemed to work.

A few minutes later, she put a finger into the brew. It was warm enough to drink as the smell of sage permeated the room. She pulled her scarf from around her neck and placed it over her mouth. Sitting on a wooden crate, she spoke to the stranger.

"Yo tea be ready, Suh."

He opened his mouth as Lucy lifted the cup to his parched and swollen lips. He sipped daintily at first, like a Southern Belle at her first tea party, savoring the soothing herbal decoction, then swallowed greedily.

"Go slow Suh, yo might choke."

The tea finished; the man fell back onto the bed as if the effort had exhausted all his reserves of energy. He flung his right arm to his side, and as it hung over the side, she recognized some deep scratches on his right arm as she rose from her seat. Her mind wandered to her experiences with diseases. The pox had infected a neighboring plantation, and the medicine man had been transferring oozing pus from pox blisters on one slave to scratches made in other slaves' skin, to prevent the pox from spreading or reducing the severity of the disease, like some primitive vaccine. Her father had gotten sick but hadn't died. She remembered getting a set of scratches on her upper arm from the medicine woman, becoming feverish for a few days but survived.

Not all had been that lucky. She hoped the magic would stay true for her (24).

Why linger in any place on her journey? This question had dogged her movements ever since she had fled captivity. Except now, she felt she had an obligation to this man. She had assisted the medicine woman on her plantation when she was needed and knew much about the uses of herbs and poultices. She did not want to remain in this cabin, but in the dark, the alternative was leaving and exposing herself to marauding rebels, slavers, or soldiers who might capture her or worse. The elements were always a factor as she listened to the wind whistling through the trees as a ragged bolt of lightning illuminated the night sky. She quickly retreated to the center of the room and felt her body tremble.

She eased herself onto the chair, leaning against its crude back, its angles cutting into hers, and for a moment, closed her eyes. She envisioned a school, sitting at a desk in a crisp white blouse and smart tunic. She imagined herself one-day teaching and standing in front of eager students as she read the day's lesson.

The first clap of thunder had Lucy standing upright and rigid. Outside trees bent under gale force winds, leaves and limbs snapped free, disappearing into the howling abyss. A whiff of Jessamine hung in the air, her favorite flower, a paradox amid the pestilence of her refuge. A buttery yellow blossom was caught on the broken pane, fluttering like a butterfly caught in a web. As she grabbed the flower, she slipped on the rain-dampened floor, hitting her head against the table and falling. Then darkness as she slipped into a dream-filled unconsciousness.

....

'Easter Sunday and the bouquet of Jessamine filled the praise house. A bible was open to Matthew and the bishop was reading the text. Lucy liked this version of the Easter story best because Jesus appeared to both Mary Magdalene and the disciples. And she loved the spring when everything was in bloom- one could dare to be hopeful amid such beauty.

She was often frightened by the Old Testament stories and remembered the preacher reading from Exodus about the enslavement of the Israelites by the Pharoah of Egypt. It was hard to believe that slavery was so old. Why hadn't God intervened and stopped the murder of baby boys? At least one boy as saved by the Pharoah's daughter. Moses. And he led the Israelites to freedom! She was told not to repeat this story as it had been removed from many Bibles by the Massas, so slaves wouldn't get any ideas about revolting (25). Her favorite story was of Daniel in the Lion's den, surviving a night amid all those hungry lions with no way out. How brave he had been. But what she loved most was to join the singing of the Beatitudes in the New Testament; they were uplifting with hopeful passages. She remembered her favorite passage.

'Blessed are de pure in heart, for dey shall see God.'

She roused briefly and shifted her body slightly, retrieving her shawl from her sack and wrapping it around her shoulders and over her head. She leaned against the wall and closed her eyes. A moment later, she had succumbed to sleep once again.

Chapter 19

Shivering and desperate to escape, Henry ran along the sandy shoreline until he reached a wooded copse of loblolly pines. He slipped into the clearing behind them, hidden from the beach, sat on a soft, fragrant bed of needles, and leaned against the rough security of a mottled tree trunk, spent.

He had seen the young girl get out of the boat, hidden beneath the tarp, and guessed she had been as desperate as he to get away from the moonshiners. He had been prepared to go to her rescue if necessary but watching her escape the sinking vessel on her makeshift raft, he had been impressed with her ingenuity. And grateful she hadn't needed his help. He had left the boat as quickly as possible; he knew men would be waiting on this side of the river of Ladies Island.

It appeared that many plantations had been abandoned by their owners once the Union troops had invaded South Carolina and supposedly freed the slaves. Some had continued to farm the land, like the slaves at the plantation he had stopped at to get food and appeared to be occupying the former Massas' homes on the Sea islands. Most slavers preferred to live on the mainland, in his experience, managing the plantations they owned there, leaving the black overseers and drivers to manage the day-to-day isolated island operations.

It was a dangerous place to be during a war. There was always a fear that emancipation could be dissolved. He was afraid of the roving bands, poor whites, and rebels that posed a constant threat. Many of the more remote islands were often uninhabitable due to disease-ridden swamps and marshes. No one could farm that land. Henry was in dangerous territory. Would he ever be able to own his own piece of land in the South? Or was that just another impossible dream? (26).

....

"Where the hell is the boat?"

"It was supposed to be here by now. George knew we'd be waitin' on him. Let's give em a few more minutes."

"I don't like it. Dem Union soldiers are all over the place watchin'. There ain't nowhere to hide this here moonshine if it ain't picked up, and we nneed the money."

In the distance, an explosion shattered the silence, and plumes of smoke were seen rising in the east across the river.

"What was that?"

"I don't know but I think we need to git outta here. I heard Johnny Rebs are hid out on another island just waitin' to attack them Union Blues. They won't much care whose side we're on once the fightin' starts. Let's hide this 'shine by that swampy water over there; we'll dig a hole, bury it, and come back for it tomorrow. George said if sumpin' went wrong, they'd return a day later."

The men retreated into the darkness and the faint sound of digging lasted for a few minutes before they fled. Henry looked around, realizing that he needed to find a more secure hiding place. If this was a regular landing area, and that was confirmed now, there would be others using it, too. It was difficult to know who to trust or who would be likely to trust him. That girl was somewhere nearby in as much or more danger than he.

The sound of cannon fire and a cloud of smoke was carried across the river on a freshening breeze and lingered over Henry like an unwelcome guest. Its scent permeated the air, its musty infusion settling indiscriminately on everything in its path, cruel reminders for Henry of the coke ovens of the mine he had escaped; Black bodies tossed in and cremated like sacks of trash. He had prayed for the memories to disappear. Instead, they had become a fearful obsession, with the threat of capture looming with every step he took into unchartered territory. Once, fire had meant warmth, family, and comfort; now, it was an evil force to be dreaded.

Henry listened for the strangers' retreating footsteps before moving. The cicadas' incessant trill returned as he headed in the opposite direction from the moonshiners, carefully choosing his footsteps in this unfamiliar territory reminiscent of the island he had just abandoned. Hunger, that constant unwelcome companion, drove him forward, pushing through overgrown highbush blueberry and prickly saw palmettos, horse sugar bushes, and ferns. It was dark and he was wary of the many poisonous berry-producing plants that were native to the low country; tempting though the berries may seem, memories of skin eruptions, boils and vomiting were lessons not soon forgotten. Sweet-smelling white and yellow flowers often betrayed their lethal character. A steady trickling ahead on his right prompted Henry to relieve his thirst at the stream. He knelt with cupped hands when a shotgun blast shattered a small tree beside him. He froze.

"What the devil you shootin' at Gabe?"

"I saw sumpin moving behind that tree."

"Well, I didn't. That sumpin' could be a rebel or a union blue. You want to get us killed. Put that thing away."

"Okay, but don't blame me if we git ambushed."

The men moved deeper into the forest. Henry maintained a tight crouch, barely breathing, waiting for a sign, of what he was unsure.

Chapter 20

Lucy awoke and shielded her eyes from a shaft of bright sunlight reflecting off a pool of water in the center of the room, a not-so-subtle reminder of the previous night's deluge. She turned her head towards the window and the sweet whistling song of a wren; its call was mimicked by another, as the pair exchanged greetings in some mysterious avian code. She pushed up onto her side and then rose to her feet. The chair lay broken by the table; the back rungs had separated from the seat, their jagged ends pointing menacingly upwards. The last thing she remembered was falling the night before. She felt some wetness in her hair and, taking her hand away, noticed a red stain on her palm. Fingering a ridge of clotted blood and probing her matted hair, she found no gaping wound, confirming that whatever injury she'd suffered was minor. No headache, a blessing.

"Water, please."

The urgent plea came from the bed in the corner, and Lucy moved slowly across the small space to her patient. His eyes closed as she gently touched her small hand to his forehead; warm, but the fever seemed to have broken. The acrid smell of sweat and hunger hung in the air. The biscuits and flask remained untouched on the adjacent table.

"Back in a moment, Suh."

She retrieved the metal cup from the floor and went to the door. The latch held, and the door did not move. She hesitated to use her weight to open it, afraid it may damage not only the door, but the jamb as well. Had someone barred it from the outside? Setting the glass on the table and the chair under the window, she climbed up onto the ledge and rested on the sill, dangling her legs against the rough exterior boards. She jumped, landing softly on the moist earth before circling to the front of the hut, where a large broken tree branch lay against the door. Moving it aside, she stared, mouth agape, at the sight ahead of her. A bold red cross was painted on the door. Arriving in darkness the night before, she had not seen the slashes. In daylight, it could not be missed. She had experienced this pox warning once before, but she had never been its target. She struggled to lift the latch, which had been damaged by the fallen branch, but it wouldn't budge. She searched the ground for a stone, found one close by, struck the wood until it offered no further obstruction, and entered the hut. Retrieving the cup, she headed towards the well, on the alert for any strange sounds or movements.

Returning with a fresh cup of water and another bunch of wild sage, she prepared the sage for the decoction as before. The candle had been reduced to a puddle of drippings; no hope of warming the tea. Still, the crushed leaves and stems should provide the needed healing effects. The man grabbed the proffered drink greedily, his hands cupping the little healer until he released her grip. He tipped the cup until the last drop passed his lips.

"More please."

The sun was rising in the east under a bruised gray sky and cloud cover that stretched across the horizon, presaging more bad weather. Lucy needed to make another foray for water, wishing there was a jug to lessen her work. Approaching the well, she heard a soft mewl coming from the charred remains of the outhouse and, out of the corner of her eye, caught sight of a tentative movement in the singed grass. She reached down and lifted a compact bundle of brindled fur. It immediately snuggled into her neck and licked her ear. She cringed, its rough tongue driving shivers down her spine. What was she supposed to do with this? She put it on the ground as a glint of light arrested her movement. Beneath the charred remains of a small table, a polished earthenware jug, an ewer, lay on its side. Except for a slightly broken handle, it was intact. She rinsed it well with water from the bucket, before filling the vessel and satisfying her own thirst. She picked sage and gathered some nettle leaves her father had used to relieve his joint pain, then turned to retrieve the cup as the cat was lapping up its contents. Issuing a soft meow, it sat up and licked its paws. She smiled at her new acquaintance, purring contentedly to itself as it stretched out on the damp earth.

She placed sage and nettle leaves in the jug, filling it to the brim, then looked about her. A broken gate struggled to remain upright while clinging to a post by a single rusty hinge; beyond it was a garden that appeared to have some root vegetables poking out of the ground. She had not had anything to eat since the day before and needed to forage for herself if she was to survive her journey to St. Helena or suffer a similar fate as her patient. She pulled up a carrot, rinsed it with well water, and bit into it, savoring its crunchy sweetness. She would return and harvest whatever other crops were available after she had delivered the water to her patient. With the little feline at her heels, she retraced her steps back to the cabin.

The man was sitting up, legs over the side and his feet resting on the rough plank flooring as she entered the room. He looked towards her; his eyebrows were raised into a furrowed brow as he stared at the young girl with a mangy cat in tow. Lucy stared back in disbelief; he was upright and appeared to have some color in his cheeks, from the exertion, perhaps.

"It looks as if I have you to thank for my recovery."

Every instinct she possessed was telling her to flee. However well she might imagine this interaction ending, her fear of capture overpowered her. She had to remain calm. He was at a disadvantage: weak, hungry, and scantily clad, making no effort to cover himself. Where were the rest of his clothes? He spoke like an educated man, there seemed to be no southern inflection that she could discern. He had a short, clipped beard and hair that needed a wash and a trim as it fell just below his ears in ragged curls. The scent of sweat and dried vomit clung to him, staining his undershirt and trousers that hung loosely from his emaciated body. She turned her head aside, realizing that she had been gazing at him impolitely. She went to his bedside and handed him the sage and nettle-infused water.

"De candle burns down so de tea be cold, but will help wid de body aches, Suh," she said with a polite nod, then quickly turned towards the door. He rose as she disappeared with the cat at her heels. He hesitated, a sudden vertigo arresting his progress, and retreated to the edge of the bed. With great effort, he rose again, moved clumsily across the rough-hewn floor, and stepped outside. He stumbled onto the uneven boards that formed the step, falling awkwardly backward as he struggled to gain his footing; then finally lowered himself to the ground, exhausted. A sudden gust of wind caught the door and shut it behind him. He turned his head.

He cringed in horror and disbelief. A large red cross loomed in front of him, like a death curse. He had heard of this mark being made to identify plague victims in the past but had not seen it in his time. He had a vague recollection of feeling ill, an overwhelming fatigue before setting out to visit the contraband camps in the area. He feared that his malaria had returned. When had he taken his Quinine dose? His last memories were of an insatiable thirst then uncontrolled vomiting. He suddenly remembered a snake- a cottonmouth- then falling off his horse and finding the abandoned cabin. How long had he been here? Where were the rest of his clothes? And where had his horse disappeared to.

He slowly rose to his feet and returned to the interior of his refuge. He lifted the cup and sniffed at its contents. Aromatic sage and something peppery tickled his nose as he tipped the cup and drank the liquid. It was slightly bitter but not disagreeable. It seemed to calm him and quench his thirst. For the first time in recent memory, he felt hungry. He noticed the biscuit and flask. He dipped one in the tea and bit into it. He was grateful for the sustenance, but realized in his weakened condition, he needed to conserve his energy until he was able to travel and return to his duties in the Sea Islands. With sudden determination, he began a methodical search of his surroundings. Luckily, he still had his shoes sitting on the floor. Kneeling, he looked under the bed and spotted the familiar silver buttons of his blue jacket. Retrieving it, he felt the pockets and recovered another piece of hardtack. He put it back on the table with the other, but hunger intervened, as he dipped it in the cup for a few seconds before consuming the entire biscuit.

His thoughts turned to the presence of the mulatto girl. Odd to have a cat with her. He questioned her presence in this remote cabin, but not her sudden departure. A runaway slave, likely. Did she know that the North had liberated South Carolina? Probably not. Some slavers were still intimidating their slaves, forcing them to join the Confederate army while killing others who tried to leave, knowing that many would join the Union forces. She was young but obviously skilled in herbal medicine. He wanted to help her, not only because of her ministrations to him but because he had a daughter of his own about the same age. Where had she gone? What was her name? Did she have parents? And why had no one come looking for him?

....

Lucy ran in the direction of the burned-out plantation house and hid behind an intact fire breast, the sole survivor of the blaze. The little cat curled around its companion's legs, silent as if understanding her vulnerability. The wind was steadily increasing, and the pendulous grey clouds promised another downpour. She could not remain here for long. After what seemed an eternity, she stood and peeked out from behind the ruined chimney. No one was in sight. The man had not followed her. No surprise there. He could barely stand. She regretted that she had fled so quickly, her survival instinct driving her. It was difficult, if not impossible, to tell who was to be trusted. Perhaps the stranger was a Union soldier who would be sympathetic to her plight and help her reach St. Helena. The fact that he had been abandoned was concerning. Even she had a companion, however recent and only a cat, but still. She had been shocked to see him sitting in bed wearing his undershirt, skin white, like bleached muslin, but with a slight yellow tinge; skinny, she could see his ribs protruding through his skin. His eyes were the most extraordinary blue, like the autumn sky on a sunny day, but red-rimmed. Kind eyes, though, she thought. Maybe he had a family too, not that that had made any difference to her Massa. Kindness had been in short supply on her plantation. She was glad she had found the jug to carry the water; it meant fewer trips to the well.

She rose and wandered to the garden behind the gate and pulled a few more carrots and sweet potatoes from the moist earth, as well as skinny green beans clinging to chicken wire. She found some hickory nuts in their shell covering the ground likely carried by the wind from a tree close by; these were dropped into her Croker sack recovered from Emma's house. After drinking again from the well, she filled her small glass jar with water and moved away from the blackened ruins and the cabin that housed the man. She made her way across the open field, skirting trampled corn stalks and colorful bluish-green Indian grass still upright and swaying in the soft breeze. The morning sun beat down on her uncovered head as she shielded her eyes, her thoughts returning to the stranger's plight. What misfortune had befallen him to be left abandoned in that cabin? Where was his home? Surely, someone from his troop would have cared for him or had a doctor treat him if one was available. She had done what little she could for his fever, having learned some herbal medicine from observation of the medicine women of her plantation; it had seemed to help, or was it simply wishful thinking?

Was he still there?

Why did she care?

Chapter 21

The sounds of cannon fire reverberated off the walls of the abandoned slave dwelling, its vibrations releasing a fine powder from the walls and patchy ceiling, coating Henry's body in a chalky shroud of grey. He coughed and hurriedly moved outside, where he spotted an ancient oak, its trunk wider than the span of his arms and its many branches forming a formidable forest canopy. Within minutes, he perched on a high spreading leafy limb, with green moss and creeping vines, screening him from detection. It afforded him a superb position from which to scan his surroundings. Across the river, as the conflict raged with rockets illuminating the night sky, he saw armed forces in a pitched battle, black men armed with rifles against their white counterparts. It was difficult to discern who was on which side of the conflict, bodies falling where they stood, in the water, on the shore and in the boats. The agonized cries of wounded and dying men were punctuated by the unrelenting reports of gunfire, deafening, unceasing and impossible to escape. Could this be the slaves he'd heard about, joining the Union army against the Rebs and White slavers? Who could survive such an onslaught? What would victory look like? After such a slaughter, could any result be declared a victory?

There was little he could do but watch, terrified. There was no safe refuge for him, even if the rumors of a freed state were to be believed. A fine drizzle had begun and was seeping through the foliage above him. He returned to the hut, grateful for the shelter, as damp as it was crude. It was empty save for a wooden crate in the corner, a slatted bed frame and what appeared to be a course blanket lying across it. The window openings had no glass, which was typical for slave quarters, but the space appeared to be relatively tidy even with the accumulated dust covering the floor. The drizzle had devolved into a downpour with vertical sheets of rain driven by a relentless wind outside the windows; luckily, its direction avoided the worst of it entering his space. Except for the odd leak, the roof remained intact, evidence that someone had made an attempt at upkeep, however humble his circumstance. A fireplace sat in the middle of one wall.

Since his arrival in South Carolina, he had seen many Plantation houses and slaves' quarters, some burned-out ruins, others simply looted and abandoned. Where he had come from, the Massas were still largely in control, and emancipation had yet to arrive; unlike these islands where it appeared that some freed slaves had occupied homes of their former Massas, while others still used their slave cabins. Not all the Sea Islands were under Union control, it appeared.

The reality of the situation was far more complicated than Henry could have possibly known. The North needed the profits from the cotton grown on these islands, considered the best of its kind in the world, to fund its massive war. South Carolina was ranked as the richest state in the Union and in the world at the time. Other countries might try to compete but came a distant second to the quality of cotton produced there. Not only was over two million dollars' worth of cotton seized by Union government officials, but much of the land had been abandoned by its owners once the North had invaded and 'liberated' South Carolina in 1861. The government seized land with unpaid taxes after a grace period had elapsed. Investors from the north and elsewhere took advantage of the cheap land too, gladly paying the taxes owing and acquiring the land at bargain prices after the federal government had confiscated over sixty percent of the sea island land for their own purposes.

Crops that weren't destroyed by fleeing residents, were harvested by former slaves allowed to work the plantations and grow food to feed themselves and the ever-expanding war effort. There were barely enough provisions for the armies; starvation and disease were widespread and took more lives than deaths on the battlefields of both the Northern and Southern armies. An average of one battle every thirty days was the norm during the Civil War, excluding skirmishes, and supplies, including munitions and uniforms, were becoming more difficult to obtain as supply lines, bridges, and roads were disrupted or destroyed. As in every war, but especially a Civil War, brother was pitched against brother, father against son, and slave against slaver. Hostility was rampant; opportunists, including Union soldiers, gleaned what profits they could from the spoils of war, some with no allegiance to either side. Spies were everywhere and it was often difficult to know what or who could be trusted. The name Pinkerton, the private investigation company established in the 1840s, was employed by the Union forces, its 'private eyes' used to infiltrate enemy lines and glean intelligence for the war.

Most people were led to believe that the Emancipation Act of January 1, 1863, would apply to all slaves when, in effect, it applied only to those states outside of the union, the eleven secessionist states in rebellion. It was essentially a wartime measure initiated by Abraham Lincoln, commander in chief, encouraged by Frederick Douglass, an intelligent, charismatic, freed black man and advisor to the president. It allowed a provision for former slaves to enlist in the Union Army and Navy; approximately two hundred thousand black men did (27). The thirteenth amendment would not be officially ratified until December 6, 1865, after the war had ended. The government of the north did not wish to alienate those states already in the union who still employed slave labor and begrudgingly paid taxes to the government, earned largely on the backs of the slave economy.

From slavery's origins in Sumar thousands of years earlier, civilizations continued to be built on a slave economy on every continent and involved almost every race; wars were fought for control of that commodity, and its brutal regime knew no limits.

One could say that Slavery was embedded in man's DNA when the first tribe, the first people on earth, subdued one another, killing the men and taking women and children hostage to serve their purposes of mating and servitude.

....

Henry hoped to find a plantation where he would be welcomed to work the land as a freed slave. The notion of a Freedmen's School on St. Helena was even more desirable if he could believe the words of the runaway slave girl.

He had drifted off to sleep when he was woken by a pounding at the door. Before he could flee, he was grabbed by the shoulders and advised he was now a member of the colored regiment.

He was led out of the cabin at gunpoint and loaded onto a wagon with several other black men, looking as confused and frightened as he.

An hour later, they had arrived at an encampment and were unloaded onto a field of thick mud. A white soldier approached the ragged group and announced they were now members of the colored infantry and would be fed and paid for their service. Within an hour, Henry had eaten, was given a union uniform, and told to get some sleep. As he lay on a cot with a full stomach, he didn't know whether to be grateful or terrified. That he was still alive was a miracle in itself.

The next day, when he awoke, he joined other former slaves and freedmen who were given guns and taught how to use them. He was holding a weapon for the first time in his life. He wondered how long he would survive in this strange new world he'd stumbled onto.

Chapter 22

The scent of smoke drifted on the wind, the sounds of musket and cannon fire slowly abating as the young, freed slave girl moved across a wide expanse of rain-saturated cotton bolls and sharp bushes. In the distance, a ribbon of teal snaked its way between the vibrant green and ochre grasses of a low country marsh. A great blue heron with its head bent plunged its lethal beak into the soft, rich pluff at the water's edge, retrieving its breakfast of hermit crabs and shrimp. The sun was directly ahead as she hesitated and turned around to take a last look at the charred ruins and cabin beyond.

'Should Uh go back ta make sholy he be alive?' Lucy wondered as she bent down and lifted the little cat, who nuzzled its brown head into her neck with a soft purr. She knew it was folly to risk staying in a strange place where the possibility of hostilities between warring factions was ever-present. She desperately needed to know the way to St. Helena, safety a secondary priority to that of speed. The forest ahead promised shade from the midday sun and its dense foliage a screen from wandering bands and rebels. She returned to the ruins, passing by the chimney breast, and was approaching the cabin when she heard the pounding of hooves and the plaintiff neighing of horses in response to the urgent commands of their riders in the distance. She crouched low behind a thick bush, straining her ears to the exchange that was being conducted outside the cabin.

"Who gave the orders to isolate me in this cabin with no food, drink, or medical care," her patient demanded, standing unsteadily as the two men dismounted and stood next to their horses.

"We was sent on patrol to find you Sir. No one knew where you was. We was just following orders from the Colonel Sir."

"I need food and fresh water and clean clothes as well as transport. Did you bring another mount for me?"

"No, Sir. But you can take my horse, and I'll ride with Sam back to camp. Take this water bottle," the soldier offered in an outstretched hand, along with a biscuit he pulled out of a jacket pocket.

"Did you see anyone else around these parts on your return today?"

"No, Sir."

"I heard rocket fire last night. Have we held our position?"

"Yessir. We believe the last of the Rebs was killed or ran. We rounded up a few and took prisoners but they was in sorry shape. The camp is crowded, and the supplies have been delayed.

The ground is a sinkhole of mud since the rains, we can hardly move our wagons. The horses are suffering somethin' bad. And rations are low, Sir."

"There is an abandoned burned-out plantation over yonder. You may find some corn stores in a barn or crops that can be harvested. Take your gunny sacks with you and see what you can find and be quick about it. I'll gather my things and meet you back here within the hour-no longer. Understood?"

"Yessir."

The men disappeared behind the cabin as the captain returned to the stoop and sat down, drained of energy. He hoped the girl was safe and would like to thank her properly, but he did not know what he would do with her if he found her. Alone, she was vulnerable to capture by slavers and rebels, or taken away and placed in a black orphanage, one of many that had sprouted up since the war had started, a war that had left countless abandoned and impoverished widows and children. Some orphanages were better than others, but money was short because of the war effort, and most resembled workhouses with education a secondary concern.

He was a lawyer, treasury agent, and an enlisted man, who worked with the troops, but his main responsibility was to oversee the freed slaves, and the schools for Freedmen that were being built on the Sea Islands including Ladie's and St. Helena. Teachers, nurses, preachers, and businessmen and agents from the North-Philadelphia and New York- had arrived and were providing support, education, and care to any freed slave who wanted or needed it. The Port Royal Experiment, it was called (28). Thousands of newly freed slaves had been subjected to horrendous working conditions. Growing cotton required a full year's labor to bring to market, with only Sundays, Pentecost and Christmas days off. Slaves spent free time on Saturdays grinding corn and tending vegetable gardens, often producing barely enough to satisfy their hunger, then sleeping a few scant hours at best each night (29). Education was nonexistent for a labor force deemed chattel akin to farm animals and equipment. Hominy, peas, and salt pork were the dietary staples, and oyster shells were often used as spoons. Smallpox, yellow fever, and malaria were constant threats. Many slave cabins, like the one in which he had been isolated, were made of rough boards and windows, most without glass, letting in the cold of winter and oppressive summer heat, with floors of sand or earth and an open hearth with a single pot for cooking.

He envisioned a better future for the young girl. She was bright and her knowledge of herbal remedies was evident even as she had to accommodate her healing art to the equipment at hand, or lack of it as it happened. She wasn't afraid of him or his disease, and likely recognized Malaria. It was a recurring malady for him, but Quinine helped. He realized that the young Mulatto girl had been fortunate to have survived the smallpox treatment and the resulting immunity, and likely the reason she was not afraid of catching the disease from him, even though he did not have the pox. (24))

Perhaps their paths would cross again. He hoped so. He wanted to help her. He pulled a field diary and pencil from his jacket pocket and wrote his name on a blank page, along with his base, Port Royal. He tore the leaf out and left it on the table under the melted candle holder. He looked over to the coverlet on the bed. It belonged to his wife who insisted he take it with him- a frivolous gesture in a camp where tents were poor refuge from the relentless heat cold and rough blankets the norm. He'd leave it. It had seen its share of use, a bit soiled and torn in spots, but still serviceable. It might provide the young girl some comfort as it had him. If not, he was certain someone else would be taking shelter here before the war was over.

Less than an hour later, the soldiers had returned. Hanging from the saddle horn on the private's horse, a burlap sack was bulging at its seams with corn and yams.

"We found some hickory nuts and chicory as well. Not enough to feed an army, but a bit of cornbread would surely be welcome.

The captain nodded and, with assistance from Sam, assumed the vacated saddle, then followed the lead horse with the two soldiers on its back. The effort had exhausted him, but he was grateful to be alive. He turned his head towards the burned-out homestead, hoping to catch a glimpse of the young girl who had nursed him through the night, but she had disappeared.

....

Lucy had watched the soldiers approach the ruins from a safe distance in the woods. They had found corn judging from the bulging burlap sack and had dug up the remaining root vegetables that she had begun to harvest before they had appeared. She had watched them drink from the well and fill their canteens before they disappeared. She heard the retreating hoof beats and, after a few minutes, returned to the cottage. She wasn't sure why she felt the need to revisit the place that had sheltered the soldier, and her for that matter, from the elements. It was more a need for closure before she could move on. She could not explain it.

She stepped inside. The acrid stench of sickness still clung to the air. The door was left ajar as she looked around the room. On the table, under the melted candle in its holder, was a piece of paper. She removed it and recognized the letters as a name but was unsure of what the remainder said. She placed it in her skirt pocket after carefully folding it. Going to the bed, she straightened the coverlet, surprised that it had been left, and checked underneath. A glint of metal caught her eye, and she recognized a brass button, most likely fallen off of the man's jacket, and something else: a photo of a family: a mother, father, and young girl, all beautifully dressed and posed. She stored those in her bag. She headed outside, making certain that the latch was in place. It had been a refuge for her and the stranger and would likely serve as one again for another escaped slave like her. The little cat was waiting at the bottom step and meowed loudly when Molly reappeared.

"Uh needs tuh get my sack by de tree den we be on our way tuh St. Helena," the young girl said as she bent down and picked up her furry friend. "Uh still has a pawpaw left tuh eat."

"Listen" said Lucy to her companion, jumping out of her arms as she walked towards the woods in the distance.

"Can yo hear? It be a Nightingale. Uh aint heard dat bird fo a long time. See? Ober der in de hickory tree. It be mimicking de little wren dat be singin' outside de cabin."

The cat perked up its ears and stared at the perch, then bolted towards it. The singing stopped. A rustle in the bushes distracted the little feline as it leaped ahead only to return quickly, grabbing its tail where a burr had attached itself. Lucy held down the squirming mass of fur as she removed the sticky barb. The cat ran off as soon as the annoyance was gone.

"Yo welcome," she said quietly to the ungrateful beast.

She reached the woods and continued along the hard-packed, uneven earth until her feet were sore and her body overheated. She sat on an old stump in a clearing thick with leaning palmetto fronds and shaggy moss before reaching in her sack for the jar of water. After satisfying her thirst, she took stock of her surroundings. The sun's rays broke through the foliage, and she thought she could see the outline of a praise house through the trees in the distance. A familiar melody. A hymn? Voices. And not just a few. Many. Had she stumbled upon a haven with people she could trust? Was it possible? She would need to be careful.

Chapter 23

The singing grew softer as she veered off the path and disappeared into the forest. Moving cautiously through the dense rain-soaked underbrush, she side-stepped fallen branches and rotting logs; she was wary of the stinging barbs of the saw palmettos that threatened to make her progress painful. A rushing stream flowed through a shallow depression in the ground strewn with the debris of countless withered flowers and leaves, pine needles, and decomposing vegetation. The clinging tentacles of a vine crept over the peaty earth towards a large marshy pond. Loblolly pines, their spindly branches and shaggy needle tufts swayed to the rhythm of a gentle breeze as they skimmed the surface of the brackish water. Lucy pushed past an ancient oak dripping Spanish moss, that cast mottled shadows onto the water as the breeze freshened. Ripples traveled across the marsh until a random branch or submerged tree impeded their progress. A dark, jagged profile just below the surface moved, almost imperceptibly, as a duck paddled across its path towards succulent water shoots at the water's edge. Suddenly, the formless shadow became a menacing maw, its razor-sharp teeth clamping down on the squawking bird, scattering its plumage into the air before settling on the roiling surface. After a brief struggle, predator and prey disappeared into the inky abyss. A ragged wreath of feathers circled the whirlpool where the victim had been swimming short seconds before.

Lucy was still. She was aware that alligators lived in these marshes and had eaten their meat on rare occasions, but the scene she had witnessed was a deadly reminder of the many perils she faced on her journey. Predators took many forms- two-legged ones posed the most immediate threat- though she hungered for a human touch and a kind word. Her little companion had reappeared, rubbing its silky coat against her exposed ankles as it laid a dead field mouse at her feet. It was promptly dispatched and served as a reminder of her own hunger. Raw vegetables, nuts and fruit did not still her stomach rumblings. She imagined a hot meal of fried chicken and okra, cornbread, black-eyed peas, and red rice. A fresh pallet with clean linens and a warm quilt were equally tempting, and she could not deny their draw. Was the possible refuge provided by strangers, fellow slaves, worth sacrificing her dream for? Could she surrender to an existence possibly more humane but equally shackled as her former captivity? Without education, was there a future beyond the field? Was it worth the risk?

The answer was a resounding no.

The scent of woodsmoke and fresh bread carried on the warming breeze distracted Lucy from her sullen mood. She stood and followed her ears; the sound of children's laughter and scolding voices grew louder as she neared their gathering place. Suspended above an open fire hung a large cast-iron pot, stirred by an elderly woman in a colorful headscarf that complimented a printed apron encircling a generous girth. Beside her, on a long wooden table, fried okra, cornbread, and yams occupied its center. Black men, women, and children were scattered nearby, engaged in varying activities, splitting wood and making sweetgrass baskets, hauling water from a well and carrying jugs of sweet tea to the table. Children chased each other, shrieking, the boys grabbing hold of one another and tumbling to the ground while the girls hid behind the trees, laughing at their antics. In the front seat of an aging weather-beaten buggy, pulled by a swaybacked mule, sat a young black man, and beside him, a skinny boy in a frayed jacket too large for his small frame. Forming a backdrop, a fading whitewashed wood frame cabin was surrounded by several tents and small cabins scattered across the property. They resembled the colored soldiers' encampment she had seen a few short days before. It reminded her of her former home except for one thing; no drivers or overseers, black or white, and no one was working in the fields. No one was cracking a whip. Could this be the freed slaves she had heard about?

She watched as the call to dinner brought everyone to the table. Wooden bowls and metal spoons were quickly grabbed and carried to the fire, where portions were ladled out of the steaming cast iron cauldron. So intense was Lucy's preoccupation with the scene in front of her that she did not hear the footsteps behind her. A tug on her skirt brought a stifled cry from both her and the wide-eyed girl looking up at her.

"Wus yo name? I'm Mary. Yo wants some stew?"

Lucy stared as Mary pulled her by the arm and led her across the field to the enormous pot where the cook was serving a small boy.

"He be my brother Thomas. I'll git yo a bowl."

Lucy felt all eyes trained on her as she reluctantly accepted the proffered bowl and spoon and stood at the back of the line. A few nods and the stranger was forgotten as each person took a seat at the table or under a tree and ate greedily. When her turn came, the cook filled her bowl and held her nose.

"Yawl bet be sittin' away from de table. When yo last had a bath?"

Uttering a thank you, she moved a good distance away under a pine tree, out of sight. Mary and her brother followed.

"Tank yo, Mary, ain yo too Thomas."

" Eh caint hear yo. Caught de fever when eh be little. Eh can read yo lips iffin yo talks slow."

"Yo lives heah in dis camp?" Lucy asked, looking around.

"Sholy do. We comes from Edisto Islan. De soldiers bring us."

She felt uncomfortable as the eyes of several of the freed slaves, gathered at the large dining table, rested on her. She ate slowly; her appetite had suddenly disappeared as nausea and thirst replaced hunger. She placed a piece of cornbread in her pocket, then stood and went to the well to relieve her thirst. Before she could pull out her glass bottle, a large, rough hand grabbed her arm.

"You be using yo own cup. No telling what sickness you be spreadin'," the tall black youth warned, as she pulled her arm out of his grip. She filled her bottle and drank quickly before refilling it.

"Weh yo from?" the boy persisted.

"Nowhere special," responded the young girl, turning away.

"Dun be boderin' my frien, cuzzin," said Mary as she took her new friend by the hand and walked towards a group of children kicking a coconut on the ground.

"Mammy has no use fo mo chilluns, Mary," the boy yelled as she walked away.

"Ah looks afta myself," Lucy replied angrily. Her stew barely touched, she replaced her bowl and spoon on the long table.

Suddenly, all activity halted as eyes turned toward an open wagon pulled by a mule. A white woman held the reins, and beside her sat a young black girl staring down at her hands. The people immediately circled the conveyance and started talking, drowning out each other as the volume increased.

"Don't worry, I have your pay," assured the slim lady who was helped from her seat by a large black man who seemed to have some authority; as the group cleared a path, the man led her to the crude dining table. The talking instantly reduced to a whisper. A bowl of steaming stew and a large piece of cornbread were placed in front of her and her companion, which they proceeded to eat while the crowd waited patiently. Molly was puzzled.

"Who be dis woman?" she asked Mary as she watched the woman take out a ledger similar to the one the Massa had used at the plantation. She called out names, and as each individual approached, he or she was handed money, carefully accounting for each in the book.

"Dat be de doctor lady, who looks afta us when we be sick ain has good medicine - helps birt babies too. De doctor talks to de soldiers ain de men who gives us wurk on de plantation."

"Weh she be from?"

"From de Nord. She come on de big ship on de ocean, tuk a long time. She be a good lady. Teach at de school too."

Lucy couldn't believe her ears. Was this the white teacher her father had spoken of? Was this St. Helena Island? As excited as she was at the possibility of realizing her goal, she was suddenly overcome with terrible nausea. She quickly turned and ran behind a nearby tree, emptying the contents of her stomach onto the damp earth. She continued to retch repeatedly before collapsing in a heap on the ground. She was oblivious to the crowd of people who were staring at her prostrate figure, pale and unmoving.

She thought she was dying.

Chapter 24

"Miss Linda, come quick," Mary called after witnessing the new arrival's collapse, running toward the table where the woman sat finishing her meal.

The doctor responded immediately; her eyes focused on the crowd standing by a tree and speaking in hushed tones to each other. Mary had grabbed her hand and was leading her to the young girl lying on the ground. Miss Linda knelt beside her and gently placed her hand on her forehead.

"She's burning up. We need to get her to shelter. Where is there an empty tent where she can rest, Amos? No one is to touch her but me," she instructed the black man who had stayed by her side since she had arrived.

"She be good in dat tent, Doctor." He pointed to one close by

"Thank you, Amos," said Linda, following Amos as he carried the young girl to a makeshift structure adjacent to the whitewashed cabin.

Lucy heard hushed voices, distant, unfamiliar. Her skin was on fire, her thirst unquenchable, as a trickle of water passed over her cracked and swollen lips; swallowing was an unfamiliar struggle. A cooling compress pressed to her forehead brought welcome relief in stark contrast to the heat radiating from the rest of her body. Her subconscious thoughts were of cool breezes and cold lemonade. Scents of sage, mint, and basil filled the air as she opened her mouth to the cooled, soothing tea that was offered.

"Once she's able to speak we'll find out where's she's from and who she might have been travelling with. She's very thin and appears malnourished, but I think she'll recover."

The woman examined Lucy's arm and recognized the series of raised healed cuts on her arms.

'Smallpox or cowpox vaccination, but at least we know she has immunity given her age, so hopefully symptoms or recurrence will be minimal if she has been exposed,' thought the woman.

She had treated several smallpox cases lately in a few of these camps. Luckily, the cowpox vaccine, first developed in the late 1700s, had been administered to the majority of the Union troops, thus preventing a full-scale outbreak in their forces. It could be fatal and, if not, took weeks of recovery with isolation, difficult if not impossible to achieve with a war going on.

She had recognized the practice called variolation, the process of transferring the virus from one patient's pustules to scratches made in the skin of another person, not yet infected.

Immunity was not guaranteed. When successful, the severity of the disease was reduced. The young girl showed no outward signs of smallpox; her mouth and tongue were free of the telltale red spots that typically appear at the onset of the disease. Her fatigue, nausea, vomiting, chills, and fever suggested malaria, and having looked after many of the slave population with similar complaints, she was confident in her diagnosis. The treatment was quinine, and she would start her treatment immediately. She remembered from her studies that it was a component of the bark from the quinaquina or cinchona tree, first discovered in the South American Andean jungle (30).

She prepared the quinine, and with some reluctance, Lucy was able to swallow it in small, delicate sips. It would take a course of treatment to relieve the symptoms, if not cure the disease and Molly would need to be watched closely over the next few days. The doctor had a number of other plantations to visit before nightfall. There had been an outbreak of yellow fever on Edisto Island before the sixteen hundred former slaves had been evacuated to St. Helena Island at the order of the Union Army. Though the Union forces were overwhelmed with finding accommodation for so many people, food and medical care was the greater challenge. Leaving instructions for the young girl's care with one of the doctor's trained aides, she prepared to leave.

A crowd gathered around the doctor, waving and shouting thankyous as the petite woman climbed up into the front seat of the wagon. As it advanced, its wheels sank into the muddy earth; the crowd helped as one, by pushing the wagon out of the rut. It jolted ahead, rising out of the mire, enabling the mule to pick up the pace. A moment later, it had disappeared round the bend in the road. The crowd returned to their interrupted meal, talking about the mysterious young girl and praising God that she hadn't brought the pox with her.

"Thomas, come wid me. Let's go see our friend," said Mary. Thomas shook his head. "Fine. I be goin' den."

Mary went to the tree and retrieved Lucy's bag. She looked around to make certain no one was watching and walked over to the 'sick' tent, as she called it. Looking inside, Lucy was sleeping on her side, and the aide was nowhere to be seen. She walked to the bed and whispered, "Uh put yo bag under de bed, right yuh, Molly. Uh be back."

She removed the now warm cloth from Lucy's forehead and soaked it in the basin of cool water before she wrung it out and replaced it on her patient's warm brow. The girl opened her eyes slowly, squinting at Mary before a tight smile brightened her face.

"Tank yo," she said weakly.

Mary slipped out of the tent undetected and disappeared into a crowd of children playing on a rope swing. When she turned back to face the tent, she thought she saw something slip under the tent, but it was gone as quickly as it had appeared. She shook her head and moved on. Inside the tent, the little cat jumped onto the bed. Thirsty, it leaned over the bowl on the bedside table and began to lap up the water. It licked its paws and curled itself into a tight ball at her companion's feet. When the aide returned the next morning, the cat was gone.

Chapter 25

When the doctor arrived back at The Oaks Plantation, she reflected on the weather and the difficulty she often faced when traveling through the sea islands. The often severe and unpredictable weather complicated life and travel for everyone: farmers, plantation owners, freed slaves, businessmen, union soldiers, and the newly arrived health care workers, who were unaccustomed to war zones. Getting supplies to the newly freed slaves at the contraband camps, like the one she had just visited, and to the hundreds of northerners who had been relocated to the sea was difficult, if not impossible, at times.

Doctors like herself and nurses who had arrived in the spring of 1862 were charged with providing care to soldiers and civilians alike in residential homes and plantation houses converted to temporary hospitals. The hub of activity was in Beaufort. Outbreaks of disease were common: cholera from contaminated water, malaria and yellow fever from mosquitoes and ticks thriving in stagnant marshes and ponds, and diseases such as smallpox for which there was often no effective treatment or cure. Due to the often lack of fresh water and persistent food insecurity, resistance to infection was low. One of the main contributing factors to these life-threatening situations was the dramatic climactic conditions.

She had been unprepared for the unpredictable weather changes in the South and had no idea how it would impact her practice here. (31) She had kept up with the news from the northern newspapers and the reports of the conflict across the country. Speaking with Mr. Pearce, she was told of unpredictable weather affecting every aspect of the conflict, from torrential rains and swollen rivers that obstructed troops and supply lines to the extremes of the Southern climate. Generals, soldiers, and civilians across the nation recorded the 'meteorological events in diaries,' realizing the critical impact of weather on the outcome of the war. Over the last year she had experienced the intense cold; this year brought heavy rains and unbearable heat. It affected crops, caused disease, and wreaked havoc on the daily lives of almost everyone. The soldiers she treated complained that the unrelenting rain caused gunpowder to become wet and made firing a weapon difficult, if not impossible, often forcing hand-to-hand combat with disastrous consequences. Following the stories in the newspapers, she read about the 1862 Battle of Chantilly during a heavy thunderstorm, where more than 2,000 men fell in ninety minutes. Many others filled the pages weekly. And so, the stories went.

The Battle of Newmarket, where Confederate soldiers slogged through a muddy wheat field, losing their shoes, became known as "the field of lost shoes." A reporter with the Army of the Potomac described chaos during torrential rains with the worst mud of the war. Wagons were buried to their axles, artillery and pontoons littered the road, while horses and mules with heads barely above the mire, exhausted from their heavy loads, dropped dead in their tracks.

In the Battle of Chancellorsville, weather worked in Stonewall Jackson's favor; the wet roads prevented the normally dry dust from being disturbed and alerting the enemy to their approach while his army marched on its unsuspecting target.

As a result, armies did not campaign during the winter from December through March, except for the rare campaign, which meant a lull in work for medical personnel and armies alike. Soldiers built log cabins with chimneys for heat, carried out picket duty, and enjoyed leisure activities such as card games and music. The Great Snowball Battle took place between two Regiments of the Confederate army in Georgia, 6,000 troops in total, and was a great morale booster for the assembled troops.

The doctor knew diseases were a constant threat to well-being, especially the soldiers, some of whom she had treated. Summer brought hot weather. One regiment reported half of its soldiers had come down with typhoid fever. She could only imagine the demoralized Union forces who had retreated to Harrison's landing due to the rain and cold amid outbreaks of malaria, dysentery, and typhoid. Heat contributed to debilitating wounds, gangrene, and skin infections; as a result, most died, not from their injuries but from diseases and infections unrelated to the original wounds.

Malnutrition was a constant struggle and had a devastating impact on the health of the soldiers. In prisoner-of-war camps, many died from diseases related to exposure, while some froze to death in primitive shelters resembling crude pens. (32)

The doctor waited eagerly for the news arriving on the transport ships from the north throughout the Civil War. Harpers Weekly and the Washington Post provided a much-needed link to the world beyond the South Carolina Sea Islands. The weather was a constant topic of conversation among the soldiers, and Captain Pearce spoke of little else when they came for dinner at the home of Linda and Etta at The Oaks Plantation. Apparently, since the 1850's, the Smithsonian Institution had established official weather recording devices. Before the Civil War broke out, over 500 stations were telegraphing weather reports to Newspapers, including the Washington

Evening Post. The war interrupted this important work. The captain and doctor had heard stories of an unusual atmospheric phenomenon called an 'acoustic shadow', which is recorded 'as having masked the sounds of battle.' Unable to identify the areas in conflict, some regiments were unable to unite against the enemy, while others were often overtaken, unaware of the proximity of their foes. On the western front in the deserts of California, Arizona, Texas, and New Mexico, the devastating heat took its toll on the armies. Not only heat but weeks of monsoonal rain caused flash flooding, wreaking massive destruction. In the east, the Navy lost the USS Monitor in December 1862 during a terrible storm off the coast of Cape Hatteras in North Carolina. The impact of the weather was undeniable.

Microclimates in states like Virginia and Maryland produced an anomaly called the 'Fog of war', especially in valleys in the late summer and fall, where visibility was reduced to fifteen or twenty feet. Antietam was the site where Union General McClellan mistook the placement of General Lee's forces. Fog rolled over the valley, providing cover for the Confederate advance, which overwhelmed the union army. The Union rallied and after twelve hours of battle, over 23,000 men, Confederate and Union troops, died in the single bloodiest day in American history. Lee retreated to Virginia and the North declared a victory. The horrific death toll, due in part to newly designed rifles fired with deadly accuracy, was second only to Gettysburg, where over fifty thousand perished over three days.

The Civil War took place during this climactic downturn that affected every aspect of the war. From planning great campaigns to building latrines for the troops, the weather was the predominant concern on every soldier's and civilian's mind. The doctor knew, having suffered from gastroenteritis and pneumonia herself, how debilitating they can be. For soldiers, adding an open wound or amputation with no definitive treatment was a death sentence. The soldiers were faced with abhorrent living conditions: wet, muddy tents, unrelenting cold or heat with no relief, insufficient nutrition or fresh water, and the ever-present danger of food and insect-borne diseases. The constant threat of attack, demoralization, homesickness, and fatigue combined to make the life of a soldier a living nightmare from which there was no awakening.

Chapter 26

Lucy was startled awake as the sound of rolling thunder penetrated the flimsy walls of the tent, she found herself in. No longer cool, she removed the cloth from her forehead and reached across to the small wooden table that held a tin cup. Sipping slowly, the tang of sage and mint eased her raw throat as she swallowed. A basin of water sat on the opposite side of the bed on an overturned crate. She dipped the cloth in it before ringing it out and wiping the sweat from her brow. Mary appeared at the entrance, stared at her sick friend, and turned away.

"Miss Linda, yo patient be awake," the young girl shouted outside the door.

Linda Townley, a formally educated doctor, entered the space and moved to her patient's side.

"How are you feeling, Molly?" she inquired, placing her hand on her patient's forehead.

"Tired. How long Uh bin here?"

"Two days. You were very sick. Can you remember anything before you arrived?"

Lucy looked at the kind white woman and was hesitant to share her story or reveal her real name. Would she be sent back to her plantation? She remembered a law about fugitive slaves being sent back to their Massas to suffer severe consequences as a result of a failed escape. As if reading her mind, the doctor replied.

"You don't have to worry about returning to your plantation anymore. South Carolina has been liberated. You are a freed slave. But I need to know what illness you may have come into contact with. Were any of your people sick when you left your home or any that you travelled with? Your mother or father, perhaps."

"Uh has no people. Uh trabel lone from de west. Uh meets a white girl on de plantation ain uh cares fo a man, a soldier I tink, who be in a cabin, yellow fever mebe."

"Good. I noticed you have scars on your arms. Did you ever have the pox?"

"Ma papa did. Uh be sick afta dey made de scratches on me, but uh gits better."

"You'll need to rest for a few more days, but as soon as the rain stops, you need to get outside in the sunshine. Do you feel like eating? I'll see if we can get you some corn bread and maybe a bowl of soup later. Eat what you can."

"Tank yo. "

After the doctor left, Mary returned with some corn bread and a cup of hot mint tea. Lucy ate the food slowly and sipped the herbal tea. She motioned Mary forward and spoke in hushed tones.

"Has yo heard tell of de School fo freed slaves on St. Helena Island?"

"Sholy have. Miss Townley ain Miss Murray teaches der. De doctor dos mostly healin' but she teach sometime. Dey's got schools on Ladies' Islan too. Yo wants tuh go?"

"Is Uh allowed?"

"Yo sholy can. Uh plans on goin' afta de harvest."

Lucy fell silent. She didn't want to wait until after a harvest, she wanted to start now. Could she ask the doctor about it? So many questions with answers she was afraid to hear. She was feeling better but had yet to stand and test her legs. Getting to the school that she'd only dreamed about was now a reality. Where she would live when she got there was a more pressing issue. This camp she had stumbled upon a few short days before might be a possibility, but the friendly welcome she had imagined from fellow slaves, freed or not, seemed elusive. What guarantee was there, that the Massas would not return? It was one thing for some white Northerners to help her fellow slaves, but it was another to imagine slaves would be allowed to stay on land they did not own. She had seen the cotton growing in the fields, gardens full of fresh vegetables and trees laden with ripening fruit, but how long before those crops would be harvested by the slaves who planted them and fed to the Union troops, or sold by the Union armies to buy guns and ammunition? The Massa had said that the cotton crop last year was the best he'd ever seen. And she knew her Massa needed the cotton money to pay his bills. She remembered him talking to his brother from a neighboring plantation, about how he might have to sell some of his slaves to pay the bills, like old man Butler a few years ago in Savannah. Over four hundred slaves, mothers, fathers, and children, separated from each other and sent away to far-off plantations, never to see each other again.

'The weeping time,' they had called it. (21)

She realized that she was no better off now than she had been before her arrival. She was thankful to Miss Linda for her white doctor's medicine and realized that she had become increasingly weak since the flight from her plantation. The bites she had suffered to her legs were likely the cause of her malaria, as the doctor had said. How many other remedies did the doctor possess?

She sat upright and swung her legs over the side of the cot. She pushed herself up and stood tentatively, one hand resting on the small bedside table. Her legs trembled, and she felt slightly nauseous but remained upright. She walked to the end of the bed reaching for its security with one hand, then returned to the head and sat down heavily. She was breathless and dizzy but satisfied that she could support herself without any assistance. Would she have to devise a new plan to reach St. Helena Island? Could she trust Miss Linda to help her? Was the doctor coming back?

As night fell, Lucy was awakened again by the rumblings of thunder shaking the sides of her tent. The canvas bulged inward with the driving force of the wind as rain seeped under the door flap. She felt a sudden chill from the damp covers and folded them back over the foot of the bed. She remembered her bag that Mary had retrieved and placed under the bed. Reaching across the table in the dark for the candle, she bumped into it with her arm, and it fell to the ground. As a flash of lightning illuminated the space, she spied the candle holder on the floor, but the taper was nowhere to be seen. She bent over the side of her cot and felt underneath for her sack- luckily, the water hadn't reached it as she pulled it onto the bed. The shawl she had taken from Emma's house was dry. She wrapped it around her shivering shoulders and rescued the last bits of crumbling cornbread from the bottom of her pocket. She placed the empty glass bottle on the table, wishing it was full. As she watched the rain pour off the canvas at the entrance to the tent, she had an idea. Rising from the bed slowly she approached the entrance unsteadily and held the bottle under the stream of rainwater, wicking off the canvas. She drank greedily, then refilled the jar and returned to her bed cautiously, not wanting to spill the precious liquid.

Once in bed, she tightened the lid on the jar and placed it on the table. The basin was on the floor, and the cup was sitting in the middle. Her shivering had lessened somewhat. That it wasn't associated with a fever was somewhat comforting. The rumbling in her stomach was a reminder that food was in short supply and remained an elusive commodity in her search for the school she longed to reach. She lay her head on the thin pillow and curled into a compact curl. A pitiful mewl came from somewhere beyond the tent. A bedraggled mat of brindled fur ran under the canvas, arched its back, and shook violently from side to side like a beast possessed, before leaping onto the bed. Settling under the covers at Lucy's head, the smell of a wet cat fused with wild sage was puzzling until she noticed the green sprig sticking to the little feline's tail. The young girl removed the fragrant herb and placed it under her pillow, its scent lingering in the air and on her fingers. After the initial discomfort of the dampness from the little animal, its warmth transferred to Lucy's body as it snuggled against her chest. Its rhythmic purring, combined with the patter of the rain on the canvas, added a strange, somnolent effect as the pair drifted off to sleep.

Chapter 27

A loud commotion outside her tent woke Lucy from an uneasy slumber. The first light of dawn slipped in through the gap in the canvas and reflected a warm glow off the glass jar on the table. She heard a chorus of hoofbeats outside her refuge before the shouting began. There seemed to be a movement afoot to enlist men in the Union Army. The discussion was heated as the slaves refused to join, arguing about the need to stay and farm the land. The soldiers threatened to destroy their encampment, remove their families, and place them in other locations, perhaps in a distant state. Lucy heard the women's pleas and the babies' pitiful crying as the soldiers continued their demands. A gunshot sounded, and a deadly silence ensued. Her mind traveled back to the day she had fled her plantation; the wailing women, the crying babies, the loud protests of the men being roped together, and the terror as the musket found its mark on her arm. She could no longer trust the doctor alone, to keep her safe.

She rose from her bed and walked unsteadily towards the tent flap. Peeking outside, she stretched her neck around the opening and saw the slaves gathered in an untidy circle. Flanking them, the soldiers stood at attention, weapons drawn. The terrified girl retrieved her belongings, stuffing her bag with the remaining hardtack on the bedside table and her shawl. She crept out of the tent, moving tentatively, fighting a vertigo that threatened her progress, away from the settlement and into the forest. She didn't know where she was headed, but one fact was clear to her now: the protection she had been promised was as fleeting as the sunny skies overhead.

As if in response to her thoughts, the sounds of cannon fire sounded, and, in the distance, an ominous ballooning grey cloud formation rose heavenward. Her body was weak, but the sudden threat of conflict had mobilized the last of her energy reserves. She rose and slipped out of the tent unnoticed. She kept a slow but steady pace until she had put enough distance between herself and the encampment to feel safe; once out of view, she settled onto the peaty earth beneath a giant oak, feeling oddly comforted by its embracing canopy. She needed to find a safe refuge to rest. Unwittingly, she once again dozed off and dreamed.

'Lucy's father was telling stories at night around the fire as she lay awake in her bunk clinging to every word about a place called 'The dismal Swamp.' It sounded like a living hell; miles and miles of swampland running south from Virginia to North Carolina before ending in some vague terminal. It was a refuge for runaway slaves or those desperate souls who had a need to escape the law or whoever might be chasing them. Whites chasing runaway slaves were terrified of going into its fetid and toxic interior where deadly cottonmouths, rattlers, alligators, and wild cats waited for an easy meal, thanks to a careless step or wrong turn. There were no signposts, and no one was willing to help anyone foolhardy enough to venture there without a guide if you could find one.

"De swamp devours ebry libin ting," her papa's words were not wasted on his daughter.

"Papa where is uh meant to go?" she cried, opening her eyes, still confused by her terrifying dream. Looking up, she saw smoke rising in the distance and smelled the acrid residue of gunpowder carried on the prevailing wind. She watched the night's rain trail off a palmetto frond. She pulled the water jar from her sack and relieved her thirst before dipping a salvaged piece of hardtack into the remaining tepid fluid to complete her meal. The exhausted child leaned back and closed her eyes before hearing a distant mewl. Looking up, she recognized a familiar brown tail appearing from behind a fallen log. She smiled as her little companion nosed under her right hand and licked her fingers, the rough tongue sending shivers coursing up her arm.

"Let's git us a place to res," the girl said, still groggy from her brief sleep as the cat ran off into the woods. She rose unsteadily and was able to move forward as the little feline led the way. She was heartened by the sight of a familiar boxy structure in the distance. In stark contrast to the verdant green of the forest, its faded whitewashed exterior and weathered shingles absent in places, spoke of an indeterminate age and very much like her praise house at the plantation. Molly approached and peeked inside through a single-glazed window. She was hesitant to enter, reasoning that this praise house might be the first place slavers would choose to claim runaways. The rain was now falling in sheets, and she doubted anyone would go out in this weather. Fatigue was once again overwhelming her, and she needed a dry, secure refuge from the elements. She lifted the latch on the door and it opened easily. Skirting crude wooden backless benches in neat rows, she approached the sturdy pulpit and lay down behind it, hoping it might screen her presence from any intruder.

"Sit a spell," she whispered to the cat as she retrieved her shawl from the bag, pulled it over her, and curled up on the floor. Her companion followed suit, forming a tight ball against Molly's warm chest. A moment later, the pair had fallen asleep. Once again.

....

Lucy had witnessed what would become a regular occurrence during the war-Union soldiers approaching freed slaves in contraband camps and attempting to force them to join their army in the fight to win the war. Slaves were also needed to plant and harvest food crops, as well as the Sea Island cotton, known as the best in the world, to fund the war. If too many male slaves were forced to join the army, it would leave only women and children to perform the backbreaking work. Complicating the situation for the Confederate cause, the southern planters had missed their opportunity to sell their harvested crops before the war started; those same profits were needed by the Confederate army to fund its battle. An anxious European market based in Liverpool and Manchester, England, would pay top dollar for it. As a result, the North was eager to sell the warehoused cotton seized after the invasion, as a contraband of War, and use the funds to fight the Confederate army. Agents and commissioners were sent by the Federal government to the Sea Islands and served many functions: to assess land values, oversee the contraband camps and the production of cotton, assess quotas for crops, distribute munitions, and perform any other duties required to sustain a war.

The newly freed Slaves were paid one dollar for every four-hundred-pound bale of cotton picked. The cost of food and other provisions was deducted from these meager wages, a deduction not generally condoned by the government commissioner or overseer. Mistreatment and misappropriation were rampant in the South.

After the war, the Union army virtually abandoned the South over the ensuing years, and many of the former plantation owners were reinstated to their antebellum (pre-Civil War) properties by President Andrew Johnson, who succeeded the assassinated Lincoln. The 'forty acres and a mule' promise made by General Sherman would not last. With no federal oversight and regulation, an ad hoc judicial system resembling Kangaroo courts, re-enslaved thousands of innocent Black men and boys on trumped-up vagrancy charges and misdemeanors; they provided the slave labor for the expanding steel industry and coal mines of the South with death rates exceeding forty percent annually, a number rarely seen pre-Emancipation. (41)

Chapter 28

Lucy blinked and rubbed her eyes as beads of sweat tracked down her face. A gentle rain had replaced the earlier deluge and continued its muted chorus on the roof, as a shaft of sunlight pierced the darkened interior, casting fingered shadows between the makeshift pews. She sat up and scanned the familiar rustic surroundings. Poised near the praise house door, her furry companion was patiently eyeing a trembling field mouse crouched in a corner awaiting its fate. Having sought shelter from the deluge, too, it must have seemed a perfect refuge until now. The young girl shivered unexpectedly despite the cloying humidity that pervaded the space. She understood too well its terror and the undeniable hierarchy of predator versus prey, the outcome predetermined. She stood and moved towards the two combatants, gathered the cat into her arms, and opened the door. The feline squirmed in protest as they watched the freed captive disappear into the forest. Perhaps this act of mercy would come back to her in kind, as the preacher had promised his congregation at her baptism, but her smile had more to do with her role in abetting the little mouse's escape than the leader's message of redemption.

Footsteps in the distance grew louder as the frightened girl rushed to the pulpit and retrieved her sack, then exited quickly, the cat in the lead. Voices in the distance were growing louder. Was this the Sabbath? She had lost all track of time as one day drifted into the next. It made sense, although praise houses were also used as meeting places. They were built small to limit the number of slaves that could congregate there. The Massas were terrified of slave uprisings, especially given the fact that Blacks outnumbered the whites at least four to one in the South; in some states the ratio was ten to one. There had been a history of rebellion; the most famous was the story of John Brown, a white abolitionist, who, with his sons and other Whites and Blacks, raided a federal arsenal at Harper's Ferry, Virginia, in 1859. Many of his raiding party were killed, including his sons; he was captured by a U.S. Marine force led by Robert E. Lee and was hanged for treason. She remembered hearing the story when she was in the plantation garden one day, and Massa's wife was having sweet tea on the verandah with her sister-in-law. She could not believe that a white man had been foolish enough to fight his own kind for the freedom of slaves. Did he not know what would happen to him? Could this be a hopeful sign of things to come? She had not allowed herself to believe it until her papa had told her that the North had invaded the islands and was freeing all the slaves.

Why didn't she feel free? Why was she still running? Why would slaves join an army where they would be the first killed when the fighting started? She did not believe that all the white slavers had left for good; surely, they would come back to reclaim their land. The dead men in the forest were traitors, but to which side? It was difficult to know who to trust. She'd heard enough bible stories to understand that there was slavery in the Old Testament, even though the slaves were not supposed to read the book of Exodus; censored editions were common in the South. Foolish, when all the slaves she knew could not read, and precious few of the bishops and preachers could. She knew most of the letters and a few words but was not literate, as the white Massas called it. Even some of them couldn't read. Slavery was as old as the Bible, maybe older. How could it end overnight? The chains and shackles may have been removed, but the lash marks on her back and those of her fellow slaves would never disappear. They ran deep, just like the roots of Slavery. 'Roots, 'she repeated to herself. Hers were in Africa, according to her father, and like roots, they remained buried somewhere in her subconscious. But she knew suffering like the black of her hand. She could recite the Beatitudes without pause.

'Blest are de pure in heart for dey shall see God.'

This was the one she had failed at miserably. She had impure thoughts all the time: thinking about how to get food even if it meant stealing, lying about her name and where she was from, moving the wasp nest near Massa's children, taking Emma's shawl and the deed to the property, stealing the boat to cross the river. She tired thinking of the endless list. She could ask for forgiveness now, but the problem was that she would likely need to commit a few more sins before she reached St. Helena. She realized with horror that she could recite more transgressions than there were Beatitudes.

"Blest are de meek, for dey shall inherit de eart.'

She hoped this one was providential. Lucy knew she was not meek, and that had cost her dearly in the past, but if it meant she might inherit at least a small part of the earth, it was worth the effort to change her attitude. She moved slowly off the beaten path until the praise house had disappeared from sight.

Relentless fatigue continued to plague her. She knew she needed more of the medicine for her malaria, but in her hurry to leave, she had given it no thought. She sat down on an exposed tree trunk and dug out her glass jar from the sack. Half full, she downed it quickly and scanned her surroundings for another water source. And food. A spreading mulberry tree leaned across a path in the distance, scraping the ground and at first glance, Lucy thought it had been picked over. On closer inspection, a low bough, heavy laden with a bunch of fat, luscious berries, dropped its fruit to the earth as she grabbed it. She stuffed her mouth with the purplish-black fruit off the limb, then gathered the rest from the ground and filled her jar before placing it in her sack. Both hands were stained a deep purple that no amount of licking diminished. Feeling renewed energy from the sweet harvest, she returned to the path, making certain that no one was following her. She hadn't seen her little friend since she had stopped but hoped it wouldn't stray far.

The bright sunshine and cloying humidity succeeded in slowing Lucy's progress as perspiration soaked through her shirt and clung to her hair. She needed to preserve her energy and reduce the need for water until she could find a refuge. A wide expanse of field opened ahead of her, neat rows of corn promising a bountiful crop. She skirted the field and approached a wide marsh, its verdant grasses swaying in the breeze that swept over the next month's harvest. She wished it were ready now.

"Dis belonged to de farmer or Massa', she thought, but no house was visible. Further along, she came to what must have been an indigo pit that yielded the treasured blue dye. That industry was abandoned when cotton replaced it as the principal crop following the American Revolution. She scraped her finger along the inside edge; a rich blue residue joined the purple stains on her fingers. In the distance appeared an outdoor kitchen, apparently a victim of a recent fire. Half the roof was missing, but the three remaining walls, constructed of tabby- a mortar of limestone, sand, and shells the slaves made, were intact. Kitchens were usually built close to the main plantation house. The chimney had survived the blaze except for its very top; it reminded Lucy of a row of broken teeth as if something had struck it repeatedly. The walls flanking it were missing, and a charred bucket lay on its side. The remaining half of the structure seemed sound and protected from the midday sun by a huge Oak, its hanging moss an additional screen from the heat, a good fire starter too, an irony not lost on the young girl. There could be a well close by, given that indigo required a lot of water to produce.

The girl moved beyond the cabin and, in the distance, saw what appeared to be a barren area. Moving closer, she was pleased to see a broken fence and a small, raised area with a wood plank covering it. She moved the plank; it was heavy and awkward, but she managed to expose an area large enough to have a good look inside. Sunlight reflected up at her. Water! She needed a bucket. Finding none, she returned to the chimney breast and retrieved the one lying on the floor. It was shattered on one side, but the bottom appeared intact. The attached rope was slightly charred, but if she doubled it, it might be strong enough to hold some water. She returned to the well. After a few unsuccessful attempts, she was able to quench her thirst; the broken side made it lighter to lower into the narrowed opening, but the effort had drained all her reserves of energy.

"Meow."

A swath of soft fur pressed against Molly's legs; she bent down and stroked the cat.

"Yo be tirsty too," she said as she lowered the bucket one more time and laid it on the ground. The cat lapped noisily until nothing remained but a bit of fur between the slats.

"Uh has us a place tuh sleep," Lucy informed the little friend trailing close behind. She moved her sack to the far corner of the cabin, which offered some protection from the elements. She spread her shawl on the charred wooden planks of the floor; she was grateful for the slaves who had used oak instead of the usual earth or sand. She had a lot to be thankful for this Sabbath as she fell asleep.

The cat sat quietly until something caught its attention in the distance. Moments later, she had returned with a field mouse between her teeth and dumped it on the floor by the hearth where it was quickly eaten. She returned to the corner of the cabin and curled into a tight ball on top of the shawl, nestled against Lucy's feverish head, purring contentedly.

Chapter 29

Linda Townley was upset a day later, when she returned to the contraband camp on Ladies Island and found many of the men gone and the women in tears. She asked what had happened and was enraged to hear of their mistreatment in what had amounted to a forced abduction into the war. This was not the intent of the Freedman's Society that was formed to create schools and hospitals for freed slaves and allow them to buy or lease land and run former plantations. Mr. Pearce would have to be told immediately but locating him would be a challenge given the large jurisdiction for which he was responsible. According to the women, there had been a black man assisting the soldiers in their mission to conscript the men and stood by, watching the proceedings after he had explained the urgent need for recruits. A handful of the younger men had volunteered after being handed a silver coin and a promise of uniforms, weapons, and three meals a day. The remaining slaves argued that there weren't enough people to harvest the crops and plant the next year's harvest. The doctor assured the remaining men and women that she would resolve the situation as soon as possible.

"I need to see to my patients and any others that need my attention. Mary, could you follow me to the tent where Molly is? She's overdue for her medicine."

"Molly be gone doctor. Run off when de soldiers come. Uh aint seen eh since."

"How could she possibly leave? She was too weak to sit up let alone run off. Did you see where she went?"

"No Doctor. By de time uh comes tuh de tent, eh be gone ain tek her tings wid her."

"I need someone to look for her. She can't have gone far in her condition. Amos, search the woods behind the tents. And the praise house. She might be there."

"Yessum Miss Townley."

"Come right back after you've searched the area. There's a marsh beyond the house so be sure to check around it too."

"Uh sholy will."

Amos returned twenty minutes later but without any news of the runaway slave girl.

"Well, she can't have disappeared. The Union army is making regular patrols around these islands. I'll tell Mr. Pierce to advise the troops to be on the lookout for her."

Mary was listening intently to the Doctor.

"Molly be wantin' tuh go tuh yo school Doctor. Tol me so. Dat's why she go'."

"Hopefully, she'll be found before then. A boat or ferry is the only safe way to another island and with all the uprisings and flooding after the rains this week it's dangerous to travel. I pray we find her before it's too late. Amos, look in the other direction."

"Yessum," the big man said and headed out on foot, a coil of rope hidden under his shirt.

Mary knew a lot about hiding spots. Her plantation house had been abandoned and then set ablaze by the Massa. It wasn't large, and the Massa was rarely there, but it was a good place to hide now, half burned, when she was tired of picking and planting seeds. Cotton was a nasty crop, and she had the scars on her arms and hands as painful reminders of their merciless barbs. She was glad the last of the cotton was harvested last year, and corn had replaced it after the Massa left. The government agent wasn't happy about it, but the soldiers were hungry, and the army couldn't eat cotton, could they. She'd never had any use from the fine island cotton; her rough clothes of osnaburg, when she got them, itched, and bothered her skin and did little to stave off the cold in winter. She would find Molly; they were kindred spirits, and like Molly, she, too, had a defiant nature. She'd rather be in school than in the fields. She grabbed two corn biscuits and a dried apple from the kitchen and headed out towards the forest.

"Weh yo goin' Mary?"

"Nun yo bidness, cousin."

"Yo afta dat runaway slave?"

"We be slaves ain we all wants tuh run way."

"Dat so?"

"Dat de trute."

"Uh be tellin' Amos."

"Tell um. Uh be Tellin yo stole his tabacci."

"Ain so."

"We sees den."

Mary turned her back and was gone.

Skirting the marsh and following a rough path through the forest, Mary passed the praise house and could see the outline of the burned plantation house in the distance. She approached it cautiously; animals, as well as rebels and bandits, took shelter there.

"Molly, wake up." Mary knelt and gave her friend a gentle shake. "We needs tuh be goin'."

There was no response from the sleeping figure leaning against the wall in the corner, a cat curled at her feet. Mary was torn; she would be missed very soon if she didn't return to camp, but she was hesitant to abandon Molly in her vulnerable state. She heard a shout in the distance and rose reluctantly, moving away from the cabin. A few minutes later, she met Amos on the path.

"Yo see dat runaway?" he demanded, looking beyond Mary into the distance.

" No Suh. Uh looks all ober, in de burn down cabin too."

"Dat be mighty strange."

He pushed her aside and progressed quickly along the path towards the ruins. Mary, dreading the outcome when he discovered Molly and realized she had lied, sat down on the ground and leaned against the trunk of an old-growth pine, thinking about the punishment awaiting her. Moments later, the large overseer reappeared. Mary rose slowly, a thinly veiled calm concealing a rising panic as she braced for the inevitable blows.

"Dat chile disappear in tin air. It mek no sense."

Mary was overcome with a confusion of emotions; first relief, no lashings today, then concern. How had she disappeared so quickly? Where had she gone? Mary had hoped to become Molly's friend, but she hadn't thought of the possibility that Molly didn't want or need her. She was sick; that much was obvious. Mary had hoped to help her get well and then go together to the St. Helena Island school.

"Uh needs tuh git back," Amos said, pushing the young girl ahead of him as he shuffled along the path back to the camp.

Lucy watched from the shelter of a dense palmetto thicket at the edge of the marsh. She was close enough to hear their conversation, but hiding in plain sight was a skill she had honed over the years. Nobody expected a slave girl to think, let alone devise clever ways of deception. Everyone expected her to run away. She normally had speed in her favor, to be sure, but she couldn't run fast enough in her condition to escape capture. Hiding had enabled her to share in the intimate exchanges and secrets of Massa's family and fellow slaves, things like crop prices, news from other plantations, weather, money worries, and debts. She knew more about the goings-on of a plantation than her Massa's wife and family, sometimes even Massa himself. She was very tired, and with her destination so close, she was desperate to go on. The people at the encampment were strangers except for one. Amos. She would never forget him. The scars on her back served as painful reminders of his lashes when he served as driver on her old plantation. Would Amos tell Massa he had found her? She had no choice. She had to move.

Her furry friend nudged her, and Lucy tried to stand but her legs felt as if they were weighted down with iron shackles as she sank to the ground. The fever had returned, and with it, her thirst. She regretted leaving the camp, but the soldiers' invasion of her 'safe' place, where she had been promised safety by the lady doctor, had been an illusion. Her head ached, and her eyes refused to focus; she stretched out on the bed of pine needles and, staring up at a cloudless sky, lapsed into unconsciousness.

Lucy did not hear the hoofbeats or the approaching horsemen, an hour later, alerted to her refuge by the pitiful mewling of her vigilant feline companion. The little cat watched her friend being carried off, then disappeared into the forest, and away from the camp and the brutality of the tall Black man called Amos.

Chapter 30

Lucy's fever had returned, and with it, her thirst. She fell in and out of a confused sleep; strange dreams of Massa chasing her and suddenly falling into a shallow marsh with crabs crawling over her and oyster shells digging into her skin. She felt her body jerk briefly; in her hands, she was holding a large rough rock and casting it at a black dog as he turned on her, leaping towards her, getting closer and closer.

She felt a cold cloth on her forehead as the cool sensation wove seamlessly into her dreams. She heard distant voices coming closer and shrank from the sound. As she opened her eyes, the figure of a man came into view. He was leaning over, talking to her, and asking her a question.

"Remember me, Molly? We've met before. I'm the man you helped at the cabin last week, Mr. Pearce. You helped me get well."

Lucy was disoriented. She didn't know where she was, the day of the week, or how she'd gotten here. Molly was her mother's name, not hers. A tin cup was offered and held to her lips. She sipped slowly before taking control and drinking it greedily.

"Whoa, take your time. There's more where that came from."

A bitter-tasting concoction followed, and Lucy was reluctant to drink it, but the man persisted.

"This will help your fever. It's bitter but it works. It's used here at the hospital"

"Where is I?"

"You are in the Beaufort hospital now. I found you by the marsh and Miss Townley, the doctor, insisted I bring you here for treatment, until you are recovered."

"Den I can go tuh school on St. Helena Island?"

"Yes, you can."

"My papa be right. The school be near?"

"Yes. There are many schools on the islands but the one you will be going to is in the Brick Church, once you are well. You will be joining with about eighty other students. Miss Townley and Miss Murray will be teaching you. By the way, I found the picture of my family in your bag when we brought you here. Would you let me keep it?"

"Shor. I be happy you found it."

"Thank you, Lucy. Your bag is safe in the closet here. You can get it when you leave."

The doctor joined the captain by the bedside.

"You are looking much better. The fever will come and go for a few more days and I have more medicine for the malaria you are suffering from. But you must promise not to run away again."

"It tek me so long tuh get heah. Uh wants tuh be a doctor too, like yo, ain fine my mama."

"I can help you with that. Mr. Pearce told me how you cared for him when he was sick in the cabin. You did a fine job with your teas."

"I do wuh de medicine woman tole me."

"We'll teach you a lot more, but you have to go to school and learn how to read and write first, Molly."

"Molly be ma mama's name. Ma name be Lucy."

"Well Lucy, let's make sure you are well enough to go to school first and find you a good home to stay in."

"Back at de camp?"

"No, close by. There's a plantation that takes in orphans like you run by some friends of mine from the north. You'll have chores to do like the others, but you will go to school every day and have a clean bed and good food to eat. Does that sound fine to you."

"Yes Doctor. Can uh wok in de garden afta school? Uh knows 'bout flowers ain begetables."

"I'm sure that can be arranged. For now, get some rest. That medicine should be working soon."

The young patient leaned back against the soft pillow. She couldn't believe that she was finally going to go to school on St. Helena. Her harrowing adventure had come to an end.

At last. Her father would have been so happy to know she was safe and with people who seemed to care about her and her future. The possibility of finding her mother was no longer a dream; they might be reunited. She was excited but careful not to tempt the spirits. She would pray for the day they would meet. Until then, she would be patient. She said a silent prayer of thanks, clasping her hands and bowing her head. She reached for the colorful bracelet circling her wrist now, her calloused fingertips comforted by its familiar security, the only keepsake of a mother suddenly and brutally taken from her. She felt tears forming, and as they fell onto the clean sheets, she started to recite the last line of the beatitudes.

"Rejoice and be exceeding glad."

And she was.

Chapter 31

Lucy checked the name of the shop with the address she had been given. 'Molly's', was etched on the sign in beautiful cursive script. The mannequin in the window was outfitted in a bright blue, indigo cotton dress with delicate white lace trim on the collar and sleeves; tiny buttons, covered in the same fabric, were stitched in a straight line onto the back of the garment to just below the waist. A pair of short white gloves and a wide-brimmed straw hat trimmed in blue satin ribbon finished the ensemble. On the mannequin's wrist hung a delicate bracelet with tiny seashells and colorful beads. Lucy peered through the window and saw a beautiful black woman showing an evening coat to an elegantly dressed white lady and smiled.

It had taken years of perseverance and research, scanning slave auction manifests, plantation log books, and newspaper ads for missing persons, as well as interviews with hundreds of freedmen and abolitionists who were sympathetic to her cause. Her discovery of the owner's slave log at Emma's plantation proved useful to many freed slaves looking for relatives they'd lost. Lucy had been able to return the gold necklace with the cross she'd found, to Emma. The biggest problem was that slaves had no last names. They adopted or were often assigned the last name of their owners like Fripp, or Butler. Some were known by a nickname or a brief description of their stature, some deformity or feature that was distinctive. She had reunited many families in her search for her own mother. Now, against all odds, she was about to realize her own long-anticipated dream of reuniting with her mother.

She fingered the colourful bracelet on her wrist, the one she had kept since she was a little girl, its tiny beads and shells still intact, having been restrung many times to accommodate her growing frame over the years. It represented a promise made to herself to find its creator; her search had finally come full circle as her eyes were suddenly drawn to the mannequin's wrist and felt a subtle shift of the earth beneath her feet.

She waited until the customer had exited the shop before she approached the door and stepped inside, a delicate chime signaling her arrival. The owner turned toward her new customer, smiled warmly then took a few steps forward to greet her. Taking Lucy 's outstretched hand, she hesitated, focusing on the bracelet. Looking up, her eyes locked on her daughters in stunned recognition.

Both moved forward, enveloping each other in a fierce embrace, as tears fell unchecked, streaming down their cheeks, the salty residue lingering on their lips. They tasted of the ocean, that vast expanse touching both home shores,

Africa and America, painful memories left behind and new ones created, more painful still.

"I never stopped looking for you." said Lucy.

"Uh knew you would find me," said her mother.

"I saw the ad for 'Molly's', a Dress Shoppe, and the owner 's name was yours. Afta all these years of searching, you live less than fifty miles 'way. I saw the notice and uh knew it was you."

"Uh has a gift fo you," her mother said as she retrieved a small box, from her desk drawer, brightly wrapped in blue ribbon. Lucy untied it. Inside, a horse-shoe shaped copper bracelet with burnished balls at each end sat on the satin lining. Molly placed it on her daughter's wrist beside the one already there.

"It's a Manilla, a slave bracelet, was used like money to buy slaves, dis one is copper, but some was gold or silver. Now we is no longer slaves, we give dem as gifs. It be a symbol of our freedom." (35)

"How long have you had it?"

"Since uh bought my freedom, it been waitin' for yo." She lifted her sleeve to expose another identical one. "Look on de inside ob yours," Molly said.

Lucy removed it and stared at the beautiful, tiny cursive etching.

"To Lucy, love Mama."

"Thank you, Mama." And the tears began anew.

They had so many stories to share: Molly, of her escape from a brutal Massa, and Lucy, her many years of study to become a doctor, working among the poor, treating disease, healing wounds, and caring for sick babies vulnerable to illnesses for which there was no vaccine or cure. She was proud to be able to serve her people, and they in turn, respected and depended on her to be present for them through sickness and health, life and death; rich or poor, it made no difference. For Lucy, they were her life's work.

"Can you stay a while" Molly asked.

"I surely can."

Molly went to the door and reversed the sign from Open to Closed.

Then, the sharing began in earnest.

Epilogue

Lucy's recovery from Malaria, like so many others, had taken much longer than anticipated, and the fatigue lingered long after the fever had subsided. The fact that she had survived at all seemed a miracle to the doctors and nurses who had heard her story and cared for her at the Army Hospital #10, in Beaufort, a converted mansion known as the Elizabeth Barnwell Gough house where Lucy had been sent to recover. It was one of many such homes being used as hospitals in Beaufort. #10 eventually served only the black soldiers; the segregation of the army hospitals began as the war continued. She remembered being treated by a woman doctor named Ester Hawke and her husband, Dr. Milton. A well-beloved nurse by the name of Clara Barton tended to her daily needs and oversaw the running of the ward. Henry, the runaway slave, was treated there and was able to meet Lucy and share his story with her. (37)

"Uh is sorry for stealin' yo biscuit. I was clean outa my head wid hunger dat dey."

"We two be hungry dat dey. Yo is a soldier now?"

"Yessum. I is a free man now an stayin' wid de army 'til uh gits de land dey promise me."

"Uh be goin tuh school. I gonna be a doctor. Mebee, I see yo agin."

Lucy's formal education had not yet begun, but she decided, before she was released, that she wanted to be a doctor and help relieve the suffering of others. Many soldiers were carried into the hospital with wounds suffered in battles on the sea islands and beyond. She was able to see the activity when she wandered through the large house, helping where she could, as she began to gain strength. She admired the skill and compassion of the doctors and nurses who cared for the wounded and dying, and it reinforced the image of herself as one of them, one day.

At that same hospital in Beaufort, Harriet Tubman, a Black abolitionist and activist who had been with the black regiment during many battles, treated and accompanied the injured Black soldiers after a terrible conflict on a nearby island in 1863. Some called her the 'Moses of her people.' She led an estimated seventy slaves north to freedom via the underground railroad, a system of trails, tunnels, water routes, churches, and safe houses of abolitionist sympathizers who assisted her in her efforts. She was a legend and revered for her courageous efforts that placed her in as much danger as those whose lives she saved on the battlefield, and on the path to freedom. (38b)

Lucy had gone to school at the Brick Church on St. Helena after her discharge and then transferred to the Penn School for freed slaves like many other children when that school finally opened in January 1865. It had been prefabricated in the north, in Pennsylvania, and shipped south, where it was erected close to the Brick church. When the Freedman Bureau closed its offices in 1870, private societies took over and aided with its ongoing work. Lucy continued her education with the assistance of Mr. Pearce, who helped her, and many other freed slaves gain acceptance to Shaw College in North Carolina, the first black college established after the Civil War. More than ninety institutions of higher learning were established between 1861 and 1900, largely funded by Black churches, the American Missionary Service, and the Freedman's Bureau. Like many others, she continued her studies at Howard University, (unsegregated- founded by the white, Civil War General, Oliver O. Howard) and received her medical degree in 1876.

Linda Townley and Etta Murray stayed on in St. Helena and would be there to watch as a New School, prefabricated in the North was erected in 1864 as promised and opened in January 1865. It was named The Penn School on behalf of its benefactor, William Penn.

"I can't believe this is really happening. Only yesterday, we were just talking about an idea for a new school, and now, look at how far we have come. Think of all the freed slaves we will be able to help." Tears welled up in the young woman's eyes.

"Yes Linda, it is a miracle. And to think we are part of it."

And they both remained an essential part of the Penn School and the Sea Islands into the twentieth century.

. . . .

The real Laura Towne (Miss Townley in this novel) continued with her mission, along with Ellen Murray (Etta Murray), her friend and colleague, contributing her own funds to support the school and work in the Sea Islands using skills both as a doctor and teacher until her death in 1901. Laura never returned North to live after arriving in South Carolina, as a young doctor and teacher; she forever considered South Carolina her home. She never wavered in her vision of a free South and the potential of its people. Many of the graduates of the Penn School went on to become teachers themselves. Laura Towne contributed more, arguably, to the education, health, well-being, and freedom of the emancipated Black people in South Carolina during her life, than any other individual and is revered to this day. In the center of St. Helena Island, near the spot where the first schoolhouse stood, stands a simple stone erected by her brother.

'In Memory of Laura M. Towne 1825-1901'
'She devoted thirty-eight years of her life to the colored people of St. Helena Island and employed her means in their education and care.' (38a)

Ellen Murray was born in New Brunswick, Canada, into a wealthy family. After her father's sudden death, Ellen Murray was sent to Europe for her schooling. She returned to Newport, Rhode Island, to teach before joining Laura Towne to found the Penn School. She remained on St. Helena, teaching there, until her death in 1908. She is buried near the Brick church under a spreading Oak. Her Memorial reads:

"Ellen Murray-A Founder. Principal, Teacher, Penn School 1862-1908

For the purposes of this story, Lucy 's life was modeled after Lucy Hughes Brown, an orphan and the first African American woman physician licensed to practice in North and South Carolina. She became an activist and a delegate of the National Federation of Afro-American Women. She became the editor of the first black medical journal -The Hospital Herald. (36)

By 1890, there were 115 black female physicians and 909 black male physicians in the United States. By 1920, the number of black female doctors had declined to 65; as did the number of white female doctors, due to sexism and racism, and the limited number of universities for women, with increased restrictions for admission. (39)

In this story, Mr. Pearce was a colleague of Laura Towne and wore many hats. The real Mr. Pierce wore many hats as well- a young Boston attorney, a Union government agent and an enlisted soldier. He was confident that the Negroes could aid in the war effort with training and education. As soldiers and farmers, he believed they were entitled to the privileges under the Constitution, but not everyone agreed. Subsequently, President Lincoln met with Pierce in Washington, and although he gave no written permission to conduct the Port Royal Project, he tacitly gave Pierce free rein to proceed with his plans. The work formed the foundation of the Port Royal Experiment, an overly ambitious project, an almost impossible job. He was, in short, responsible for the successful integration of the newly emancipated Blacks, as productive members of society through educational and vocational training. In addition, he was tasked with overseeing the housing and land ownership, of thousands of freed slaves seeking safety, amid a brutal civil war. (33)

Author's Editorial

How can one human being, a human soul, be possessed by another? The idea of slavery, of one people subjugating the freedom of another, boasts a horrifying longevity. It has thrived since the Mesopotamian and Sumerian civilizations (6000 to 2000 BCE-The History Press), the birth of Islam, Buddhism, and Christianity, and continues to this day in many countries throughout the world.

One has only to think of the children, over 160 million worldwide, some as young as five, working in brick factories in Thailand, in rice paddies and fields throughout Asia, in India, and even the USA, many as indentured workers living in squalor supporting their families while receiving no education or health care. (World Vision 2021). How has this situation evolved in a supposedly enlightened global society? Economics, greed, power, Industrialization, displacement, land appropriation, civil unrest, and war all contribute to the slave economy, one predestined to impact the most vulnerable global demographic: children.

This is a work of fiction, but it takes its inspiration from real events and real people. There is a plethora of history books on the American Civil War and the North American slave trade dating from the sixteen-hundreds, from an educated, sometimes biased, and often white male perspective. In contrast, there is a dearth of information from their counterparts, black men and women. Why?

The answer is simple. Most never received an education because they were slaves and as such, treated like chattel: cattle and farm equipment. They were hobbled, shackled, beaten, maimed, burned, and whipped, often until unconscious or dead. Many were killed when their efficiency waned, after a failed escape, or succumbed to untreated diseases, physical abuse, and starvation. Entire families and offspring were regularly separated and sold to other plantations, often never to see each other again, arguably the cruelest torture of all.

The Sea Islands of South Carolina form the backdrop of this story. The isolation of these Islands along the eastern seaboard, of South Carolina, Georgia, and northern Florida allowed the 'Gullah' and 'Geechee' cultures to survive and thrive, a culture that included a unique 'Gullah' language, a combination of Creole, English and with African influences whose authenticity was first pioneered by Dr. Lorenzo Dow Turner in the 1930s and others into the twenty-first century. (1)

Religion was often based on a Methodist model combined with black magic, hoodoo, and voodoo. Herbalism, root doctors, medicine men, and women provided an essential healing art, as medical treatment was rare to non-existent for slaves. Herbal and root remedies were often administered to and used by white plantation owners and their families. Distinctive island cuisine uses locally grown ingredients, especially corn, rice, root vegetables, okra, and beans. Black drivers, appointed by white plantation owners, were often left in charge of the day-to-day operations on the sea island plantations. The reason? The whites were terrified of succumbing to the various diseases that were endemic to these islands: malaria, yellow fever, and others for which there was no effective treatment or cure. Some evidence suggests many of these diseases were brought to the Americas on the slave ships that plied the Atlantic Ocean.

Black slaves were thought to have immunity to many of the mosquito-borne illnesses, but many succumbed to these diseases. Sickle cell disease was the 'trait' carried by many black Africans, providing significant immunity from malaria due to the altered 'sickle' shape of the hemoglobin molecule. Other blacks, who carried the sickle cell 'gene,' were as vulnerable as anyone else to the deadly disease. Most children died early from it, often before their second birthday.

Rice, cotton, corn, tobacco, and indigo formed the main crops that were harvested. The Slaves came from Western African countries including Angola, Sierra Leonne, Ghana, Liberia, Gambia and Senegal, and were not randomly chosen. They brought with them the knowledge of rice, cotton, and corn cultivation from their native lands. Sold into slavery by black African tribal leaders, their story of abandonment and enslavement started long before they boarded the overcrowded, suffocating, and disease-ridden vessels bound for the Americas. In 1800, an estimated eighty percent of the African population in continental Africa was enslaved. The slave economy thrived in Africa, as tribal leaders used them as their main source of wealth and income. When slavery was outlawed in 1808, one tribal black leader asked an American slaver, 'Where do we get our money from now?" (11)

Africans weren't the only slaves: Indigenous peoples, Asians, and blacks from the Caribbean islands were also subjected to the misery of captive labor, often forced off their deeded and native lands and sold into slavery. In Florida, many indigenous people were used as slaves long before the Atlantic slave trade to North America from the west coast of Africa and later sent to mines as slave labor along with the blacks.

During the early days of the North American slave trade prior to the eighteenth century, most slaves were brought to the American South from the Caribbean islands. The Sea Island cotton industry replaced indigo as the most profitable crop, after the Revolutionary War with England, approaching the nineteenth century. In contrast to indigo, many more slaves were required to do the yearlong backbreaking toil of the planting, weeding, and harvesting of cotton; they were imported on slave ships to southern ports like Charleston and New Orleans. The slave trade, though declared illegal throughout the colonies and Europe in 1808, and abolished in 1838, served as little deterrent to plantation owners who depended on the Sea Island Cotton to build their plantations and make their fortunes. The law would take years to be effectively enforced as Sea Island cotton continued to be arguably the most valuable crop in the world until the American Civil War. South Carolina was considered the richest state in the world due to its cotton production. At the outset of the Civil War in 1861, the Union consisted of thirty-five states; nineteen Confederate States, of which eleven were secessionist, and sixteen were Union. The North desperately needed the profits from cotton sales as well as other contraband of war to fund their efforts to reunite the union, including the eleven secessionist states.

More slaves were born in the American South after 1808 than were imported and bred much like cattle, often sired by white slavers, to populate the plantations for the cultivation of 'King Cotton.' In 1800, one in ten slaves was born in the United States; by 1860, the percentage had increased to one in four. Young children, some under the age of six, were employed in the picking of the crop. Not only black children but white children as well. Almost eighty percent of the population in the American South were impoverished white farmers. Today, in Uzbekistan, children are still being forced to work in the fields with their parents, many highly educated, under a repressive political regime. (Human Rights Watch).

The most tragic fallout of the Emancipation Act and the Reconstruction Era post-1865 was the re-enslavement of young, mostly black men, subjected to another forced labor, arguably more brutal and restrictive than their ancestral chains, in the coal mines and steel mills predominately of Alabama and the American south. (34)

The Civil War was the deadliest war in American history; over 600,000 died in conflict, more than the WW1 and WW2 combined (digital history). The war bankrupted the South, killed, and displaced thousands of its residents: Blacks and Whites, rich and poor, enslaved and free; painful emotional and physical scars persist, and an abysmal political rift that shows no sign of resolution today, more than one hundred and fifty years later.

It is an unimaginable and despicable epilogue to a war that divided a nation, a desperate and tragic commentary on a so-called enlightened and emancipated America. (42)

The cemetery in Shiloh, Tennessee, speaks louder than any global antiwar propaganda.

The most significant impact of modern warfare since the turn of the twentieth century is that civilians now outnumber soldiers and other combatants, among the dead. It is documented that between fifty and seventy million civilians died in those wars, including the most vulnerable-children. The numbers continue to rise in the twenty-first century. Simply stated, war is an act of genocide, a fact that is still being debated around the world. Its impact on the global climate cannot be understated. Just as the world fostered slavery for thousands of years for economic gain, the global community can no longer afford to ignore the undeniable outcome of continued armed conflict and the destruction of life as we know it and its impact on global climate change.

Change is going to come in one form or another. It is not too late to reverse the rising tide of conflict and human exploitation. The survival of our world and that of future generations depend on it.

Keeping history alive as a deterrent for future conflict is necessary. Around the globe, war museums, libraries, and veteran organizations, with their worldwide networks, are constantly updating their records while those working to maintain these documents provide an invaluable service by preserving the memories and lessons of war. The simple reality - War is a battle for survival. No glory. No winners. In War, the most precious and essential of human qualities is lost.

Our Humanity

References

1.Gone with the Tide'–Pearce Hammon-pgs 30-39

A Study in Gullah as a Creole Language-Nora F. Abdou-http://www.hrpub.org/pgs 58-64

2-Snake Spotting-Tony Mills-Herpetologist-The Spring Island Trust

3-Quilt Codes-Smithsonian Ctr. For Folklore>folklife.si.edu

4- 'Beatitudes'-The Holy Bible-St. Matthew- Chapter 5

5- The Reconstruction Era'. The National Park Service Handbook-Foner et al

6- Sweetgrass Baskets>thecharlestoncitymarket.com

7- The Sumptuary laws- jstor.org-Duplessis-South Carolina Slave act of 1735'.

Slave cloth, Negro cloth, and plantation cloth sold to slavers for clothing were coarse and inexpensive. Jean cloth of cotton or with wool weft twill, was supplied to be made into sturdy clothes for slaves doing field work. Clothing was a mark of social status. On some plantations, slaves were allowed to grow their own cotton and ship it north to be made into cloth for their own use. Qualities such as Osnaburg, and Kersey were for lower ranks of society; several qualities were available, the cheapest for slaves and a higher grade for artisans and tradespeople. Indigo blue jeans made of wool were considered a fine article for Massa and planters' suits, made by a manufacturer in Rode Island. Racial discrimination knew no bounds; clothing represented the most visible evidence of social repression.

8- Gullah Cultural Legacies - Emory S. Campbell pgs 24.34 Gone With the Tide-Pierce W. Hammond-pgs 51-54,89-93

9- The Reconstruction Era-Official National Park Service

10- Slavery by Another Name-Douglas A. Blackmon-pgs 43-47

11- The Slave Trade-Hugh Thomas-Chapter 28

12- Gone with the Tide-Pierce W. Hammond-pg.51

13- Slavery by Another Name -Douglas A. Blackmon

14- Emerging Civil War Part 2-Valuables'

15- Croker, Crocus Sac/Gunny Sack > ahdictionary.com

16- Battlefelds.org

17-National Geographic issue<May 2102-Civil War Battlefield Art-pgs. 44-56

18-Dysentry-battlefields.org

19, 20- Southeast Foraging-Chris Bennett

21-Weeping Time-Slave auction-1859-www.nps.gov

22- Letters and Diary of Laura M. Towne-1862- Intro-pgs. X1, X11, X111

23- Gone with the Tide-pgs 51-53

24- royal society.org

25-The Holy Bible-Old Test.- Exodus -Ch 6, Daniel Ch.6

26-Rebellion, Reconstruction and Redemption-Forty Acres a Mule-Stephen. Wise and Lawrence S. Rowland. pgs 386, 622

27-eji.org>equaljusticeinitiative

28- see (26) pgs.66-75- and Rehearsal for Reconstruction-the Port Royal Experiment-Wilee Lee Rose-pgs 22-26

29-Letters and Diary of Laura M. Towne

31, 32-Little Ice Age-1310-1850-EncyclopediaVirginia

33-Letters and Diary of Laura M. Towne-pgs. 50-53

34-Slavery by Another Name-University of Oxford and PBS Special on the Civil War and Reconstruction

35-Manilla-Principal Currency in African slave Trade-Ashmolean.org

36- Dr. Lucy Hughes Brown-wwwscencyclopedia.org

37-ClaraBarton-Rebellion, Reconstruction and Redemption S.R. Wise and S. Rowland-pgs 205,206, 248,249

38a-Letters and Diary of Laura M. Towne

38b-www.womenshistory.org

39a.-Louis Calder Memorial Library-University of Miami

39b-Property-owning Free African American Women in the South- 1800-1870 Schweninger

'Many Free Black women and former slaves had bought their freedom and those of their children and indeed owned property, city lots, businesses and buildings and tracts of farmland. In Petersburg, Virginia, forty to fifty percent of freed Black women owned land. Interestingly, black women were probably just as active or more so in the market economy than men, selling such things as crops, tobacco, livestock, and baked goods. '

Many examples existed of Black women who ran plantations and owned slaves, such as Ann Johnson and Madam Cyprien Ricard. In 1850, in the Lower South, among the 10,123 adult free Black women, 561 were listed as 'realty owning heads of households. Between these free Black women, they owned $1,671.400 worth of real estate.

In the 1850s free Black women controlled a substantially larger share of Black wealth than white women controlled of the white wealth. Several hundred of these free Black women lived with propertied white men and shared, in part, their wealth and accumulations. Many inherited their partner's estate, even though they were not legally married. Often, these same women refused to enter marriage because if the marriage dissolved, then her land holdings and personal wealth would be ruled by the courts as the property rights of men through marriage. (#38)

40- Contraband Camps-International African American Museum and southernlibguides.com

After the Union army occupied South Carolina and the Sea Islands in 1861, declaring emancipation of the enslaved people there, plantation owners fled, abandoning their plantations and lands. Thousands of slaves were left essentially homeless. Many of the plantations, buildings, and land that had been razed by both landowners and the invading Union army were now occupied by newly freed slaves and those 'affiliated with the Union forces. The U.S. considered these freed slaves as contraband of war, 'akin to captured enemy property such as ammunition, houses, horses and the like.' They were supported by the union government with food and education and were paid wages as farm laborers. They existed in many of the Southern states, and the men often became part of the colored militias, albeit unwillingly, in some cases. The women often provided services as cooks, laundresses, nurses, and custodians, aiding wherever they were required.

41-Slavery by another Name-Douglas Blackmon

In lieu of a state prison system, a bankrupt South could ill afford, the steel and mining companies provided 'accommodation' for the 'prisoners,' and their system of control was often brutal. The conditions were arguably worse than on any antebellum plantation; because they were no longer slaves with an assessed monetary value, they were worthless, could not be sold, and deemed expendable. Subjected to poor food, backbreaking working conditions in rat-infested mines deep underground, and little exposure to sunshine or easy access to clean water, torture, disease, and malnutrition were rampant. Since there was no benefit to the owners of the mining and other industries to keep the former slaves healthy for the slave block, this endless supply of free, mostly Black labor continued to thrive well into the twentieth century.

42. Wealth and Culture in the South-US. History-OS Collection- OER Services- Cotton is King- Antebellum South.

"As the wealth of the Antebellum South (pre–Civil War) increased it also became more unequally distributed, and an ever-smaller percentage of slaveholders held a substantial number of slaves." (sic).

Nathaniel Heyward, a wealthy rice planter, sat atop the pyramid of southern slaveholders. In 1850 he owned more than eighteen hundred slaves and an estate of over $2 million dollars, more than $63 million in 2014 dollars. Seven of the first eleven presidents owned slaves.

In the white Class Structure of the South in 1860 approximately 0.1 % were slaveholders like Heyward with 100 + slaves, 6.6 % had under 100 slaves and 17.2 % had less than 9. 76.1 % of were non slaveholders.

Below the wealthy planters were the small land owners called yeomen. Below these were poor landless whites who made up the majority of whites in the South. Despite the obvious unequal wealth distribution, it appeared that most white southerners were bound together by a common belief system. They did not support an active federal government and were suspicious of the State bank, and did not support taxes meant to create railroads, canals and other infrastructure- to them all government represented was interference in the natural workings of the economy and what they viewed as essential and rightful slave ownership. The Honor Code of the South was all about control of dependents, not only slaves, but wives, children and relatives. It was in effect a 'pre-capitalist' system, where feudalism and serfdom formed the foundation of their economic and social lives. The desire to maintain Antebellum roots and the Confederate constitution would continue in the steel mills and the coal mines of the Reconstructionist South and beyond, so much so that Mississippi did not ratify the Emancipation Act until 130 years later, in 1995, and was not officially filed until 2013.

About the Author:

Cheryl Miles is a published author and a member of The Writers Union of Canada. Born and raised in Montreal, she moved to Toronto to complete her nursing education. Her family roots lie in a small, isolated Newfoundland outport on the Atlantic Ocean where she spent many summers visiting her extended family. The self-sufficiency of the people there, who made their living off the land and from the sea, has remained with her and influences her writing. The South Carolina Lowcountry and the unique qualities and resilience of the Gullah people are reminiscent of her own ancestry and fueled her interest in the history of Slavery. As a mother and grandmother, she often writes from the point of view of a child- powerless, and dependent- one who sees the world through the lens of an innocent- unedited. A history buff, she spent six years researching how the Civil War impacted the lives of Sea Island people, especially those of the most vulnerable - Children.

Since retiring from her nursing career, Cheryl has channeled her time and energies into full-time writing and her business as a professional artist. Nature- forests, waterfalls, oceans, and wildlife, especially birds- feature largely in her art.

Her first novel in the trilogy-Bella and Dash – 'The Forest'-was published in 2018 and is available on many sites, including Amazon and on her website. The second, Bella and Dash-Down Under'-is due for publication in 2025. The third in the series- Bella and Dash-The Savannah-is in the planning stage.

Two Romantic Mysteries, Loose Change' and 'The Homer in the Attic"-are completed and awaiting publishing in the 2025.

Cheryl is currently completing a short story anthology about the lives of endangered animal species around the world.

She lives in Burlington Ontario, Canada, with her husband Rick, and has four daughters, three stepdaughters, and six grandchildren. A cat lover, one is often featured in her novels, a tribute to her pets-Ollie and Kiwi.

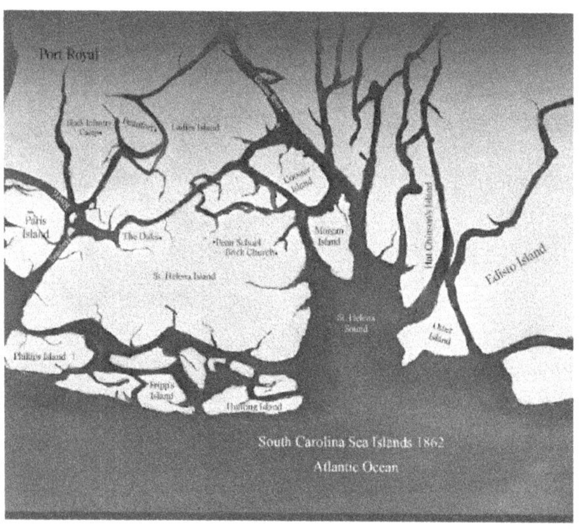

Port Royal
Beaufort
Ladies Island
Beaufort Camps
Black Islands
Crocker Island
Paris Island
The Oaks
Penn School Brick Church
Morgan Island
Hut Chisom's Island
Edisto Island
St. Helena Island
St. Helena Sound
Otter Island
Phillips Island
Fripp's Island
Hunting Island
South Carolina Sea Islands 1862
Atlantic Ocean